COURTING
RENDITION

COURTING
RENDITION

Social unrest. Political intrigue.

Calculated injustice...

MAGGIE ALLDER

Matador
9 Priory Business Park
Kibworth Beauchamp
Leicestershire LE8 0RX, UK
Tel: (+44) 116 279 2299
Fax: (+44) 116 279 2277
Email: books@troubador.co.uk
Web: www.troubador.co.uk/matador

ISBN 978 1784621 520

British Library Cataloguing in Publication Data.
A catalogue record for this book is available from the British Library.

Typeset in Aldine by Troubador Publishing Ltd
Printed and bound in the UK by TJ International, Padstow, Cornwall

Matador is an imprint of Troubador Publishing Ltd

MIX
Paper from
responsible sources
FSC
www.fsc.org   FSC® C013056

To my parents Brenda and Tony,
who gave their children love and security,
and the freedom to be ourselves.

CHAPTER 1

I'm settled at the open door of my Juliet balcony, looking out on the garden below, thinking how much I love Mondays, and feeling a huge surge of contentment within me. The sun is still very low, the trees are casting long shadows over the grass, and there are dead leaves on the lawn, a reminder of the winter to come. Soon, though, it will be bright and sunny. I think I will walk across the park when I go into work later today. The children will be back in school now, their uniforms clean and new, the teachers mostly rested and enthusiastic, the mothers off to work, if they have work, sighing with guilty relief that their children are out of their hair. I think I will walk the long way through the park, by the river, where there used to be picnic tables under the trees until the council moved them at the beginning of the summer. There were two or three tents there when I walked past with Sky last week, and we wondered if we were seeing the beginning of a tent city. It is not a good place for homeless people to set up camp, it's too obvious and too many public-spirited citizens, less devastated by the changes in our society than those setting up camp, are likely to see and object. On the other hand, it is a convenient place, close to town and especially to the feeding centre down by the bridge, and if there are any children there they might be allowed into the local school. Sky, who works Fridays and Saturdays at the centre, told me that somewhere in this area there are now over two hundred homeless families, and that the two schools which have been taking them are overwhelmed, and looking for ways to refuse new applicants.

The wonderful thing about Mondays is not that I have such an enjoyable day ahead – an hour or so of housework, a walk into town for early lunch with Jo and then an afternoon at the charity shop – but that I don't have to go to work. Okay, I call my various volunteer activities 'work' but they are not, and compared with life at the chalk face (although it was really the whiteboard face long before I retired) it is all so stressless. We get some pretty awkward customers at the charity shop, it's true, and recently it has been hard dealing with threadbare people who want to sell us their cast-offs instead of donating them, but it is nothing like the worry of anxious and assertive parents, Ofsted inspectors, performance management and, in my case, increased suspicion directed towards me because of my all-too-public opposition to the direction in which we could all see the country is going. I had ceased to be the ideal teacher some time before I left.

The contrast between Mondays then and Mondays now is huge. It starts when I wake up – because my body wakes me up, not because an alarm insists that I open my eyes. It continues with a slow breakfast eaten comfortably over a good book – or uncomfortably if I'm reading, as I increasingly do, about the effects of recent legislation on the poor. Then I write this journal, and that is the biggest difference of all. For the first time since my student days I have time to consider each day at the beginning, thinking about what it might contain, holding it, as my community says, in the Light. It calms me, writing things down. I think I am less reactive than I used to be, more prepared for what the day might hold. Karl is concerned about my journal. If I were using my DeV47 he would be even more worried, but even these handwritten books make him anxious. I don't know if he has ever read any of them. It wouldn't surprise me if he has (he might read this in a few days or weeks, for all I know) but he has asked me to be careful, not to use people's names, not to exaggerate my opposition to current trends in society, not to be too radical. It is hard to take Karl's warnings seriously. I was born and brought up in this country, I have lived here most of my life, I find it difficult to believe that by expressing outrage about government policy or alliances with disreputable foreign powers, I might be putting myself or anyone else at risk. Yet I do know that certain left-of-centre websites are being discredited in many ways, and there is a campaign against the perceived bias of all sorts of media organisations, especially what is left of the BBC.

Karl is one of two mysterious men in my life. No, I made a firm decision when I settled to write the first page of my first journal two years ago, that I would not exaggerate or be melodramatic. I do have a streak of melodrama in myself, I know. It is only partly true that Karl is mysterious. That we should be friends at all is probably the really odd thing, but we have been friends now for so long that it seems natural, even though it was so unpredictable.

Karl, of course, is politically opposite to me. He works in one of those uniformed organisations which is neither police nor army. I have no real idea about what he does, although he insists, if we ever get anywhere near to talking about it, that he is involved in saving this country from forces which would destroy us. Karl is not a right-wing fanatic. He is an intelligent man, definitely brighter than me, with a quick grasp of situations and a phenomenal store of general (and not so general) knowledge. He read politics and economics but his knowledge of history (which I read) is greater than mine. I never see him read the classics, he reads all the time but usually it's detective novels, yet he can talk about any author and almost any book.

I don't often see Karl in his uniform although he was wearing it when we first met. There had been some trouble with two of my Year 10 boys. The school was never told what had happened, but we were contacted by the ATTF and asked to make an interview room available. They were in my year group, so it was my office which was used. Karl was not one of the interviewers, he arrived afterwards, when the parents had come in and they had all – boys, parents and interviewers – left together. Karl had come into my office and asked if he could just check some facts from the records. He was wearing a khaki uniform, very smart, and a peaked cap of the same colour with a deep blue band round it. There were lots of shiny buttons, and shiny black shoes which should have looked wrong with the khaki, but didn't. I was disinclined to trust Karl. The whole ATTF thing was very new and there was a lot of discussion on radio, TV and on various blogs about civil liberties. We didn't need an anti-terrorism task force, so the argument went, we needed a fairer society. I suppose Karl was charming, but not in the sense that the romantic fiction I used to read in my teens suggested. He looked around my office as if he were genuinely interested in the pictures and documents I had on the walls and on my desk, and he asked me questions about my photography before he asked to see the kids' files. I had been taking pictures looking through windows or doors, I was interested in transitions from dark into light, and from cool to warm. I remember one of my pictures was taken from inside a church in rural Brazil, looking out at a very hot, sun-bleached square. Karl seemed to know a bit about Brazil, we talked about the way Roman Catholicism was being challenged by new religious movements coming in from America, and how it might affect their politics. Then Karl looked at the kids' files, asked to have some parts printed off, and left.

I need to be careful. This journal is not here for me to reminisce, but to work through things in the present, and to help me to live a more focussed life. I will spend a few minutes in silence now, trying to concentrate on the goodness I see all around me, then I will hoover the flat.

Tuesday September 6th

Yesterday gave me a lot to think about, and I am glad to be sitting here with this rather nice pen in my hand, and time to reflect.

I hoovered right through the flat, even the spare room which doubles as an office for me. I have come to really like it here, although I had some doubts when I moved. I always thought that eventually it would be sensible to relocate to somewhere without the steep stairs of my last house, but I had no intention of moving

4

quite so soon. I had just retired, and I feel more fit and healthy now than I have felt for years. Then these flats were built and Sky and I decided to look around them, and it just seemed ideal. I thought I might miss my garden, not because I am a very good gardener, I'm really not, but because I so like sitting outside. This flat is upstairs (there is a lift but I refuse to use it while I can still use the stairs, which could be for years, even decades yet) but I have French windows onto the Juliet balcony and free use of the garden, which is maintained by a couple who come in once a fortnight and chat together in some Eastern European language all the while they work. I bought the flat early last summer and discovered, to my great delight, that when the leaves fell in the autumn I could see all the way across the park. My view from this living room reflects my state of mind – or is it heart? Full of peace and a sense of space.

Anyhow, once the flat was clean and I had checked my emails, I set off as planned the long way round the park, to see if there were still people camping in the far corner, under the trees. The answer is that there are. I think there were three, possibly four, tents there when Sky and I first saw them last Thursday, now there are six and some shelters made of plastic bin liners and other bits and pieces. There was a washing line strung between the trees, with children's clothes flapping in the breeze, and there was a pile of plastic containers and beer bottles against a tree trunk. There seemed to be nobody around, the tents with zips were closed up and there were no voices, but a dog growled from inside one of the makeshift dwellings and it looked as if there had been a camp fire there recently, by the river.

I wonder how long the authorities will put up with this, and I wonder what, if anything, I should do. I would like to talk to Sky, but I won't discuss this by any electronic means, bearing Karl's warnings in mind. The thing is, I don't know what they do with people like those campers nowadays. For most of my working life the rules said that homeless families had to be housed. The homeless single were always more vulnerable, but if there were children or old people involved, local authorities were obliged to act. Our school

5

catchment area didn't include many people who were this unfortunate, but after the first decade of this century we did see a few families get into real difficulties. I remember there was someone in Paul's year whose family were moved away to be housed in a bed and breakfast somewhere. Paul wanted the kid to finish his education with us but of course the parents couldn't afford the bus fare back out to our school, and the local authority wanted the child – I think it was that ginger-headed boy, Simon – to go to his local school. I rather suspect that Paul would have paid the fare himself, but they had just introduced those anti-corruption rules to prevent teachers from tempting 'desirable' students into our schools to boost our results, so his hands were tied. Not that most people think that homeless children from destitute families are all that desirable!

Of course, I have seen homeless families before, or at least families who are virtually homeless. Last summer I caught the train down to the coast and I was just sitting, looking out of the window, when we flashed past one of those little railway buildings you see beside the tracks, a little Victorian brick-built hut with a slate roof, right by the lines. We were past it almost at once, the train was a fast one, and I just saw almost out of the corner of my eye that there was a child playing right outside the scratchy green hut door. It was a bit of a jolt, the child was small, maybe three, and the hut was only feet from the railway line. It made me look more closely, and during the rest of the journey I saw that at least two and possibly three of these tumble down shacks were occupied. I can't imagine that they have water or power supplies, but at least those families have roofs over their heads.

I've mentioned this to a few people since, especially at Meeting, but nobody else seems to have noticed what I've seen, and everybody knows there's a huge problem with the gap between the rich and the poor, so my conversations don't seem to go anywhere. People at Meeting are, of course, doing lots – campaigning, donating to housing charities, the Walkers have even housed a family in their granny flat – but none of those things help me to know what to do now. If I contact the authorities, what will happen to the families? I have heard that some official bodies take the children away from their parents. Is it a criminal offence to camp in the park? It wouldn't surprise me if the adults were to be arrested for vagrancy or something like that. Plus, I don't know who these people are. They could be Travellers in which case I think they would just be moved on. Or they could be 'undesirable aliens', who would then be deported to some country even less sympathetic than our own, and where the children don't even speak the language. Should I buy some food and take it to the people in the tents? But anything I do will just be a drop in the ocean. It is September, soon it will be winter, they can't live in those tents and leaky plastic shelters in December or January or February.

I need to come back to the things I know. I really believe that it is wrong to act until you are clear about what you should do. I am going to stop at this point, and ask for guidance and direction. If I hold myself open to whatever is best for me to do, then when a chance comes to do the right thing, I hope I will see it and take it.

Today will be another pleasant day, I think. I need to get my ironing done this morning, because Jo and Fran are coming after lunch to knit squares with me. It's odd, this square-knitting. We started it last summer at a conference where we were encouraged never to sit unproductively, and we rather enjoyed it. We give our squares to the nuns at St. Agnes', they make them into blankets and send them off to developing countries. If you had asked me before that conference, I would have said that knitting squares was one of those things people used to do way back in the 1970s. I'm almost sure I knitted them when I was a Girl Guide. It was a bit of a surprise to learn that the nuns still do it. Fran, Jo and I meet once a week nowadays, to knit squares and talk. Fran has an almost endless supply of wool because she knits for the whole of her extended family. It is such a lovely day today that I think we will sit in the garden. I think I might tell them about the tents in the park, too. This evening I want to watch the Mull movie on TV.

I had a letter from Simon yesterday. Simon, of course, is my other mysterious man, but again I am really exaggerating. He and I have been writing for four and a half years now and I have been over to visit him twice. There is a lot I don't understand about Simon, but that doesn't so much make him mysterious, as it does make the system under which he was condemned totally unfathomable. He has been on death row in Texas for nearly ten years. It is said he murdered a man, and it is said he planned it in advance and that it was an unusually vicious assault, but the evidence seems amazingly flimsy. To be honest, I've spent hours talking to Simon, two separate trips to Texas despite the increasing difficulties in travelling over there, four visits each trip, four hours each visit – thirty-two hours of talking. It took me months to do that much talking with Karl. In some ways I know Simon far better than I think I might ever know Karl, and I really cannot believe he is guilty of murder. I would find it hard to believe he could be guilty of anything, in fact, beyond the use of profane language or maybe a speeding offence. I know Karl thinks I am being naïve, but I learnt to trust my instincts years ago, and nothing has happened since to make me change my mind. The mystery with Simon is why he was arrested and how he was ever found guilty. If I ask him, he changes the subject. Of course, when we talk we're sitting with bullet proof glass between us, using telephones which can be monitored at any time, but why would he mind the prison officers knowing how or why he was set up?

I think Simon sounds depressed in yesterday's letter. His wife stopped writing several years ago but he has two children and Maria, the elder, has always been good at staying in touch. Simon tells me in this most recent letter that he has not heard from her for six weeks, and that last time she wrote she told him she was dating some guy who Simon does not trust, a man much older than her. I can't work out whether his main worry is that Maria has fallen into bad company, or whether he is upset because she's stopped writing. Or it could be both. I find myself in the same situation I was in when I saw the tent people on Monday. I don't know what, if anything, I can do. I have Simon's wife's address because for the last two Christmases I have sent the family Christmas cards, but I can't write to Maria and tell her that her father is missing her. It would be a shameful intrusion into their family life, and a really busy-body sort of thing to do. I suspect, if Maria is like most seventeen year olds, it would probably be counter productive too. So once again all I can do is hold the situation in the Light. I don't think of myself as an activist, but I wish I could do something about these situations.

We had a lovely afternoon knitting, although I didn't talk to Fran and Jo about the tent people. Jo brought her neighbour, Sabina, who has a two-month-old baby, a beautiful child with dark hair and eyes, wrapped in a saffron yellow shawl and gurgling peacefully between being fed on demand. We knitted our squares and talked about air travel, and how the new green taxes have affected Sabina's husband's employment. It seems he used to go away on a lot of short trips, then come home and have long weekends to recompense him for all the time away from his family. Now they try to roll the trips into fewer but longer excursions, and he comes home tired out, jet lagged, and with lots of paperwork still to do. Sabina, meanwhile, is struggling with their first baby, with not going out to work, and with not having any family nearby. Reading between the lines, I would say that she is leaning on Jo a bit. Jo will love that, she likes to be needed.

It was warm, too, yesterday. We sat in the dappled shade of the big trees in the corner and I served fruit juice as well as tea. These September days can be so lovely.

Today is a bit cooler. There was a mist blurring the view from my living room window when I got up first thing to make coffee, and although it's cleared now (just after 9.00am) there is still that autumnal smell in the air. I am sitting with the French windows open. I can't remember how long I continued to be able to do this last year. I suppose I could look back through my journals to see, but I'm not sure I mind that much. I am aware that I don't have quite the same settled contentment in my mind – or is it my heart – today. I have a jumble of feelings and I can't untangle them. I think

I am disappointed because I didn't dare introduce the topic of the tent people yesterday, I hoped that, having held it open in my heart in the morning, a way forward might become clear in the afternoon. Then the Mull movie in the evening made quite a big impact on me. Mull is a very perceptive novelist, and the film is, as far as I can remember the book, pretty faithful to the original. It deals, as all Mull's books do, with corruption, intrigue and political shenanigans, and I found it gripping, convincing and frightening all at the same time. When I turned out my light I found that I couldn't stop thinking about it, feeling angry with the idealists who are driving us ever further right, deceiving people, convincing them of dangers that don't exist and of rewards that will never happen, allying our country with forces of greed and selfishness around the world, and ruining lives. Karl would say I was being melodramatic again. I turned the radio on to try to distract myself, but there was a history programme about Christmas Island during and just after the Second World War, so then I felt angry about the corruption back then, too.

I think I also feel guilty because I am going over to Karl's for dinner this evening. Oh dear. This crops up again and again and I really don't know what to do about it. I am tempted to think I should just hold this in the Light too, but all this holding of things in the Light seems more like procrastination in my present mood.

Well, let me try to focus on the day ahead. We have mid-week Meeting and lunch today, an uncomplicated and peaceful occasion to which I look forward. I do a short shift at the shop until around 4.00pm when I should be replaced by a college girl, then I'll come back here, shower and change, and catch the bus over to Karl's place. Of course, I'm looking forward to it quite ridiculously.

Thursday 8th August

I feel tired but content this morning. Karl has a surprisingly small flat considering that he must be really well paid, and I stopped sleeping in his bed years ago. The settee converts into a bed that is generous and comfortable, but somehow I always take a long time to go to sleep there, and I wake often. My visit followed the usual pattern. When I arrived he was cooking, lovely smells issued from the kitchen and he had some popular music on his sound system. I have never caught Karl listening to the radio (except when there's a cricket commentary) but somehow he knows what is going on in popular music, and every now and again he downloads a CD or a few tracks of something all the kids are listening to, and plays it over and over again for a few weeks, before dropping it entirely. I wonder how he is introduced to these groups or singers. Where does he go, to become acquainted with teenage music?

He had subscribed to two films, and gave me the choice of which one we would watch. I like it when he does this. Sometimes we channel hop through hundreds of equally boring programmes. I, of course, favour documentaries and historical dramas, Karl likes quiz games, cookery programmes and fly-on-the-wall shows about immigration or about the lives of airports. I chose a Bollywood film, a romance based very loosely on *As You Like It*. It was beautifully done and we both enjoyed it immensely. It is unusual for Karl to watch a whole film without once checking his DeV47, but he did so last night. Ridiculously, it made me feel I mattered to him. When he starts sending and receiving messages I feel I am unimportant, and that he has forgotten I'm there. Yet we've known each other for nine years, and he still invites me over. I suppose my insecurity stems from all sorts of uncertainties, about who Karl is, about his work, and about the whole of the rest of his life, where he goes, what he does and with whom.

This morning Karl was up before I was awake. That's the usual pattern. He was wearing jogging clothes and looking fit and tanned. He drove me home, he said he was going on to his gym. I dare say it was true.

Another reason why I feel good today is that Meeting yesterday rather took me by surprise. We are, primarily, a group which is experience rather than doctrinally based, but I share the reservations of many about actively looking for those experiences. The only right way to approach worship is to look for Truth – Truth within, and then Truth from beyond us. If a person has an experience, that is good, but not something to hunger after, to envy in someone else, or to focus on. I went to Meeting feeling a bit down. To be honest, if I were not in the routine of going I might have given it a miss, but that is one good thing about routines, they serve as structures to stop a person from slipping into inactivity. Anyhow, I settled down quite quickly and with a lot more ease than I might have expected, given my lack of enthusiasm yesterday. There were about a dozen people there. I know the faces of all of them, and the names of most. We are a strange mix, people who are disillusioned with mainstream religion and people who are fed up with mainstream politics, joined in silence.

Usually nobody speaks at all in these Wednesday meetings, and when they do speak, nowadays, it is in quite a cautious, reserved way. These meetings are open, anyone may come and we do not necessarily know much about each other. There is such strong sympathy for the right in our society now that some of us have become careful about what we say. I cannot prove it, but I am pretty certain that my known political sympathies caused some of the trouble I experienced before I retired, and I was probably partly protected by my friendship with Karl. We have heard of public employees who are made redundant when others should have gone before them, and of allegations, made but never proved, about people once in influential positions. The internet keeps up a constant stream of such reports, but somehow the truth never comes out. It is all rumour and hearsay.

Not that I was thinking about these issues yesterday. There is usually a flower arrangement on the table, but yesterday someone had made a display of autumn leaves. There was a twig with green leaves, some yellow and brown, and a stem of bright red maple leaves. The effect was stunning, and I started to think about the perfection of the created world. Even now there is so much variety, leading to so much beauty. I started to think about patterns and about timing. I don't know what sort of tree the green leaves came from, but I suppose that tree sheds its leaves later than the tree from which the gold and brown leaves had come. When would the maple leaves drop? Each would fall at the right time, making endless quiet change in the natural world.

Then Leicester stood to speak. He said that he had been thinking about John's Gospel, about the disciples who asked Jesus where he was staying, and Jesus answered, 'Come and see'. Leicester explained that he had been thinking about that statement, 'Come and see'. He explained that his family has been divided by an argument for years, because his son moved in with a guy the rest of the family didn't approve of. He had been thinking about this, and realised that unless he visited his son in his home with this guy, he would never know first hand whether his son is happy, or whether the rest of the family are right thinking that the other guy has taken advantage of him. Leicester said that there is a principle in 'Come and see', that we should not depend on rumours but that we should see for ourselves before we make up our minds.

At once I saw that this applied to me. Or rather, I *felt* it applied to me, with an almost physical certainty that seemed to go right through my body, sweeping my low spirits away. I saw that I have to go and visit those tent people. Before I can know the right response to their circumstances, I have to know what those circumstances are. Somehow, too, it tied in with what I had been thinking about the leaves. I can feel very urgently about things – here are people living in tents, I should do something about it at once. But the leaves fall each at the right time. There is order in our world, even despite what humans have done to it. Acting on the problem of the tent people must only happen at the right time, and first I must go and see for myself.

I have made up my mind, therefore, that once I've written this journal and written to Simon, I will walk into town, to the post office, going the long way round the park, and if the tent people are still there I will look for a chance to stop and talk to them.

It goes without saying that I haven't told Karl anything about this.

It is raining, a steady even downpour, old-fashioned rain that waters everything without causing flash floods. It has its own beauty, a sort of evenness and calm. It is cooler today too. Later on, when I've come back from the shop, I think I will look through my winter wardrobe. Of course, there are two quite separate reasons for doing this. One is that I will soon need my warmer clothes, the other is that I might take the clothes I no longer want, not to the shop as I normally would, but to the tent settlement.

As planned, I walked round that way yesterday. First I wrote to Simon, a difficult task because he had sounded so down in his letter. What can I say to a man who is warehoused as he is, in solitary confinement, and waiting to be executed?

Well, I have an approach which usually works, and once I got started the letter almost wrote itself. I long ago realised that life is full of small interesting details. Once, for example, I was walking to church (this was before I gave up on formal religion, or it gave up on me) and I saw a Brussels sprout in the gutter. It was peeled, all the ragged, dirty, outer leaves were gone, and there were two knife cuts through the top, the way I have always prepared sprouts for the pot, and there it was, lying in the gutter. What was it doing there? Had someone carried a paper bag of prepared sprouts along the street, and somehow dropped one? Had a dutiful daughter, visiting an elderly mother, brought the sprouts for Sunday lunch and knocked the bowl over in the car, so that when she opened the door, this one rolled into the gutter? Had someone in one of the houses had a row with his partner, and thrown a sprout which went sailing out of a window? There had to be a story behind it. On another occasion I was walking through the town very early one morning and there was a man standing at the corner of two roads, where the farmers' market is nowadays, with a white owl standing on his shoulder. He politely wished me a good morning, and I did the same to him, then continued on my way. The owl stared at me, unblinking.

So I started my letter to Simon telling him about the leaves on the table at Meeting. We rarely write about religion, but writing about a display on the table is fine. Then I described these early September days, and what it is like to go blackberry picking, and about home made blackberry wine. All these things will seem very foreign, even exotic I think, in Texas. I described the spare room and the efforts I had made to keep the door open so that the room is aired, and how in the end I had placed a teddy bear as a door stop. I told him about sitting knitting in the garden, and about Sabina's baby, and that reminded me of a funny conversation we had in the hairdresser's a few weeks ago about mothers wanting hair cuts for toddlers, and in no time I had covered a couple of pages which will, I hope, take Simon's mind from his grim situation for a few minutes, and make him smile.

It was about eleven in the morning when I left the flat. There was quite a strong wind yesterday and I was wearing my green jacket and jeans. The grass in the park is quite long, they don't cut it as much as they used to because of spending restrictions, and there is the beginning of a pressed-down footpath where people walk their dogs. I followed that until it turned right, and I kept going as if I were just doing a full circuit of the grounds. The tents were still there, in fact there might even have been more of them. Two dogs were tied to a tree and they growled as I approached, but they didn't bark or pull at their leads, trying to reach me. Then a child came out of one of the plastic shelters, a boy of maybe four or five years old wearing shorts and long socks, and a sort of poncho thing in blues and greens. "Hello," he said, quite brightly.

His mother came out as I answered. She looked less friendly than her son, but not aggressive. Wary, I would say.

"Can I help?" she asked, in exactly the same tone I would use in the shop if someone had been looking along the rails of second-hand jackets for longer than seemed reasonable.

For a minute I didn't know what to say. All my reservations about being a busy-body came back to me and I felt silly. Didn't these people have enough to deal with? Before I could answer, the woman, who really looked more like a girl because her hair was in a plait down her back and she was wearing no make-up, spoke again.

"We're not doing you any harm. We wouldn't be here if we had anywhere else to go."

"No," I stumbled, "I mean yes. You're not doing me any harm. I came to see if I could help."

The girl looked at me a minute. The little boy moved over to stand close to her, pressing against her legs, and she rested her hand protectively on his shoulder.

"I shouldn't think so," she said. "Unless you have a spare house we could move into, or a whole lot of money."

I felt stupid. What had I expected her to say? "No, I'm sorry," I said. "I just thought ... well, do you have enough money for food? And winter clothes?" I looked around their site. It looked quite welcoming in the sunshine and shade, with the wind in the trees and the river still quite low, and clear as glass. "It'll start to get cold soon."

The girl sighed. "Well, that's kind of you," she said. "But I doubt if there's much you can do. We have all the clothes we can store at the moment. There's nowhere to keep anything dry, you see. And Peter's bringing in a bit of money, and with that and the Feeding Centre we can still eat. I don't suppose we'll still be here in the winter. We thought they might have housed us already, but they say there's a waiting list ... we're hoping... Peter's always worked, since the day he left school, although it's short hours now, of course, and we've always paid our taxes. We thought ... but they say there's no more money for temporary housing, and the lady who filled in the forms said we were irresponsible to have started our family so young." She looked more sad than angry. "My mum said the same," she added.

Then the expression on her face suddenly changed. "I'll tell you what," she said, then paused. "Are you ... do you really want to help or are you one of those people who came yesterday evening. The ones who want us out?"

"No, I really want to help," I said, thinking that if local people were already making a fuss I was sure their eviction would come soon.

"Well, they won't let Jamie into the school," the girl explained. "It's just across the park, we can see it from here, but they say this is not their catchment area. Of course, it isn't any school's catchment area, because there aren't any houses here. And we haven't got any books. I should have thought to bring some when they threw us out, but it all happened in such a rush, and the men were arguing with Peter and I thought he might hit one of them, and Jamie was crying. We just took what we could pack in twenty minutes. They said we had been given enough warning ... Could you get me some books? I'd like to help Jamie learn his letters."

So I agreed. I went on to the post office, posted Simon's letter, and then dropped in at the shop. I knew there was a good collection of children's books there, and I bought half a dozen, and a nearly new teddy bear with a flag on its jersey (Brazilian, I think, so it can't have been all that new. How long ago were the Brazilian Olympics?). I walked back the way I had come and handed them over to the girl, and felt, as I let myself in the front door of the flats, that I had done the right thing. I thought that if I had just taken some winter clothes over there, as I had first thought, it would have been a useless gesture. It was as Leicester had said, first I had to go and see, then I would know what was the right thing to do.

I need to keep holding that little family and their situation in the Light. I wonder if there is more we should do, and what it might be? I need to ask for guidance and at some point I need to talk to the people in my Meeting. It is almost a whole month before we have another Business Meeting, but I wonder if I might go to the elders? Only once again, I am not clear in my mind about what is right.

Meanwhile, today is a really straightforward day. I'm working at the shop from ten until two, I'll do my grocery shopping on the way home, and it's my book group this evening. It seems unfair that I have such a good life when Simon is where he is and those tent dwellers are in the park, and it's raining... Nevertheless, I do enjoy each day, and I am thankful for it.

When I was working, Saturday was the only day that I had a lie-in. I often used to go to Karl's on a Friday evening, and on Saturday morning he would bring me breakfast in bed (we were a proper item then, more or less). There seemed to be something so luxurious about not having to catch that bus into work. Even now Saturdays seem special although really, of course, they are just like any other week day except that there are more children around. This morning is a rather grey morning, not raining but with a blank, monotone sky. The woman upstairs (Judy, I really like her) has her grandchildren each weekend and I can hear them running across my ceiling – well, Judy's floor. I sometimes think I have missed out by not having children of my own. I never really wanted them, it's part of the reason I'm single now, but when I hear Judy with her grandchildren I do think it sounds fun.

I slept badly last night. I hardly ever sleep really well, but the book group upset me. I think Sky is working at the Feeding Centre today. I want to try to see her.

Whatever I do, I need to fit it round swimming and dinner. When I first retired I had the feeling, as I just wrote, that Saturdays should be special, but that tended to make them into anti-climaxes. By then Karl's friendship with me had moved on and we were seeing each other less often, and all the chores I used to try to cram into Saturdays in order to keep Sundays free, either no longer needed to be done (like my marking and preparation) or I did them on different days (like my laundry). Then when my brother died and Amy, his widow, moved down to a village a few miles away to be near her grandchildren, it changed again. I never much liked Amy. No, I have vowed to try to be honest in this journal. I thought she didn't like me. She is a potter, a round, chaotic sort of person who speaks bluntly in a voice I associate with the Home Counties, and with money. She and DD, my brother, raised three happy, confident kids who each in turn went off to university, met ideal partners, settled down in pretty villages with good schools down the lane and village shops and churches, and set their sights on living happily ever after. Meggan is the middle of these three paragons, and Amy chose to live near her because there was an old forge for sale in the village (I can't believe it can have been a forge for at least a century now) and Amy thought it would make an excellent pottery.

I heard these plans in one of those circular letters that appear in your inbox round about Christmas. I only read it out of fondness for DD, who had been a reliable and friendly sort of brother, but when I realised how close Amy would be, I emailed back and said we should meet up some time. I was really surprised when she took me up on it, and even more surprised when we met up for lunch in a pub here, and talked and laughed all afternoon, so that first we had lunch, then we sat in the pub garden (in February! But it was a very mild day!) for afternoon tea, and finally Amy suggested we had been there so long we might as well have dinner too. Now we meet up quite often, but on a very irregular basis because of the demands made on Amy by her children and grandchildren, her village church (which she appears to have taken over), and some charity she is involved in which seems to meet in the House of Lords, and does something to help Eastern European immigrants get involved in the arts. One of the things I really like about Amy is that she is so accepting of the things I do. She acts as if all her associates have a friend on death row, a vague and indefinite relationship with a member of the ATTF, work in a charity shop and belong to a politically suspect religious group with no creed. She asks me questions now and again, but not the sort of questions people usually ask. For example, she might say, "Which state does Simon come from – is he a Texan?" but she's never asked, or even hinted at, whether I am in love with him, which is the sort of question the secretaries at school or my dentist might want to know. She once asked me who Karl's commanding officer is, but when I said, "I don't know," she patted my hand approvingly and said, "Quite right too!" (Actually, I really don't know. Until Amy asked, the question had never even occurred to me.)

Our most recent venture is to do with keeping fit. Amy thinks we should take up swimming, but as there is of course no sports club in her village, and Meggan's pool is so small you can only play in it, Amy suggested we meet here, have a swim, and then have dinner. I rather suspect that the dinner might undo the healthiness of the swimming, but it is a good idea, and so we are meeting at 4.00pm ('Adult Swimming Only. Lanes. Non-Swimmers Please Use Learner Pool').

Since I am meeting Amy for swimming I will need to see Sky earlier, and that doesn't work very well. The main meal at the Feeding Centre is between midday and 2.00pm, and the volunteers start work at around 10.30am. Sky, who is a staff worker, does the food shopping earlier, so on Saturdays it's really hard to get hold of her. In the past few months they have been struggling to source enough food for everyone who turns up and 'food shopping' seems to involve a lot of negotiating and some begging – all very time consuming. My plan, decided upon in the early hours of the morning, is to ask if I can go with Sky in the electric van, so that I can talk to her on the way. It is because of the book club, of course.

I never got into the habit of reading newspapers. I don't even recall our household taking a paper when we were children, and beyond a brief flirtation with a respectable left of centre broadsheet when I first started teaching, I have never taken one as an adult. For a while I subscribed to several online, but in term time I didn't have time to read them, and I came to depend then, as I do now, on the radio. This works well in most ways – I feel I know what is going on, not as well as Karl does, of course, but at least as well as most people at Meeting. The big weakness in my present arrangement is my grasp of local news. Local papers bore me, with their reports about Boy Scouts going on exchange trips to Louisiana or the local recycling bins being vandalised on a Saturday evening. Every now and again, however, there is something which crops up in the local paper and I miss it. This is what happened yesterday.

We have the book group in Sarah and Andrew's house. It is usually a gentle, sociable meeting of about eight people, although technically I think twelve of us are members. Andrew, who used to teach English Literature at the university here, chooses the books.

He has a strange method of selecting our reading material: Andrew goes online to see what can be downloaded for under fifty cents, and we vote between those books. It sounds odd but it has led to an amazing range of good books. Last night we were to discuss Charles Dickens' *Barnaby Rudge*, which I had not read since the sixth form.

When we arrive there is always a slightly stilted few minutes while people take off their coats and jackets, look around the room to see who is there, and make polite conversation. Then Sarah starts handing out glasses of wine and nibbles, and the social ice is broken. It was at this point last night that Jodie asked, "Has anyone seen the correspondence in the *Messenger* this week about the tent city?"

" 'Tent city' is a bit of an exaggeration," said Andrew, who was taking a cork out of a bottle. "We walked over there this morning. There can't be more than a dozen tents."

"Well, 'tent hamlet' then," corrected Jodie. "According to the *Messenger* it could turn into a city. The local authority won't have any more money for rehousing until next April, and rents are bound to go up before then."

"How do people get into such a mess?" groaned Freddy. "This is not a poor country!"

"No," I agreed, "it's not. But it's a country with poor people in it. And rich people."

"Don't start all that talk about equal distribution again!" Freddy was getting upset. "If everything were distributed exactly equally today there'd be rich people and poor people by the end of the week. Some people just don't know how to manage their money – or their lives. They need to take a bit of responsibility!"

"What did the letters in the *Messenger* say?" asked Jim, who had come in just as the conversation started. "Indignant of Mariner's Hill?" Mariner's Hill is a rather wealthy part of town, with large houses and one or two helicopter pads in back gardens.

"More or less," said Jodie. " 'Scroungers litter public park' – that sort of thing."

"Well," said Freddy, who had gone red. He doesn't live on Mariner's Hill, but his rather large house is in Cathedral Walk, which is almost as good. "I wouldn't want to look out on a bunch of layabouts camping ten feet from my garden, leaving their rubbish everywhere, attracting rats and probably using drugs."

Andrew had a handful of peanuts. He was eating them one by one, slowly, as if each had its own delicate and unique taste. "Where do you think homeless people should go, Freddy?" he asked, mildly.

Freddy's colour darkened. He was sitting with his legs crossed on Sarah's basketwork chair by the window. He started to tap a foot on the ground. "I dare say if they used their initiative they could find somewhere," he said. "Family, if they haven't fallen out with them, or they need to get back together with their husbands and wives. When people's marriages break up they think they suddenly have the right to two homes instead of one – at our expense, of course. Or maybe they just need to be satisfied with smaller houses. We can't all have a bedroom for every child, you know."

Andrew and Sarah exchanged glances. In his mild sort of way I could tell that Andrew was angry, but Sarah was wearing a 'don't go there' look on her face. She said, "We've got some Swiss biscuits here. Our youngest brought them back from her summer school. Try them, they're really good."

Jim was getting interested. "I don't really think people would live in tents because they were holding out for three bedroom houses!" he pointed out.

"There aren't any three bedroom houses," Jodie said. "Or two bedroom, or one bedroom. The *Messenger* sent a reporter to the housing office, and interviewed some people in the queue. There aren't any houses at all. That's what the letter writers are so upset about. The Council is actually sending people to the park. They have nothing else to offer."

"Ridiculous!" exclaimed Freddy.

"Shocking," murmured Andrew.

"Appalling!" proclaimed Jodie, and took another biscuit.

"They're going to be there all winter," I thought. "I have to do something."

I think the last two days have been quite productive. For a start, I caught Sky before she left for her shopping expedition on Saturday, so she picked me up in the van about half an hour after I'd finished my journal, and we drove to the cheaper supermarkets to the south of the city. It was interesting watching Sky work. The managers of both supermarkets know her and one of them is certainly sympathetic. Sky buys things that have reached their sell-by dates, or which are on special offer, but at the second supermarket they also gave her stuff – food in battered packaging or dented tins. We collected quite an assortment of items, and it was not clear to me how the Feeding Centre would be able to make it into one large meal, but Sky was confident. "Soup or stew," she declared. "It covers a multitude of sins!"

As we were driving back I told her about the tents in the park, and about my strong feeling that I ought to be doing something.

Sky is one of those matter-of-fact people who seem to treat life's unfairnesses as a given, not something about which to get indignant, just something to deal with. I have never heard her make a political comment, although I am sure her views must be similar to mine, and I don't think I have ever heard her express outrage, which I think I am in danger of expressing all too often.

"Yes, of course we knew about those people," Sky said. "The first family put up their tent nearly two weeks ago and they've been coming to the Centre ever since. We're trying to convince the local authority that they need to contribute to our costs, if we're going to feed them, but they say it's an illegal encampment and they don't have any responsibility."

"But they're sending people there!" I could hear the indignation in the tone of my voice, slightly hysterical compared with Sky's even speech.

"Not exactly," explained Sky a little wearily. "From what we've been told they mention the camp is there, and they probably drop a hint that they might not be moved on if they settle there, but they don't exactly send them there. It's all done with hints and vague comments. The people in the camp have no security, because if public opinion gets too stirred up the Council or the police will have them evicted, but in the mean time the Housing Authority has a strategy which stops people from just camping outside their offices. And you know, the Council really has no money at all."

I told Sky about taking books over to the girl I had spoken to on Thursday.

"Well, that sounds like a good idea," Sky said, brightening a little. "It bothers me that all those kids are out of school, it's just a vicious circle. If they grow up without an education then they'll only be able to get bad jobs, they'll be poor, they'll run the risk of homelessness, and there we go again." She sighed. "It was like that even when things were better."

Swimming with Amy was also a lot of fun. Amy wears a floral swimming costume like something from the 1950s, but she's quite a good swimmer and we did our thirty-two lengths, which is half a mile. Afterwards I cooked dinner – pork chops with a mushroom and garlic sauce and mashed potatoes with leeks in them. Amy beguiled me with stories about the village, her grandchildren (Josie seems to be dyslexic, but very bright) and her Eastern European immigrants, who are putting on some sort of show on the South Bank at Christmas. She also told me a story I had not heard before, about the first time she took DD home to Guildford to meet her parents, and DD's car broke down. I remember that car, it used to break down about once a week, but DD was still a student then. He couldn't afford to have it mended at a garage and he was always useless with mechanical things. It seems DD bonded with Amy's father over the carburettor and they were friends for ever after. We drank a bottle of red wine, which was fine for me, since all I had to do was go to bed, but Amy happily took the lift downstairs, got into her car, hooted the horn a couple of times and drove away, well over the limit. I dare say if she were stopped by the police she would mention the name of the elected chief constable – she's bound to know him – and be let off with a warning.

Sunday was normal. By that I mean that I went to Meeting, had coffee afterwards, chatted about insignificant things, and walked home along by the river. There were several visitors to Meeting – there often are nowadays. I vaguely knew one of them, my neighbour from before I moved. She said, afterwards, explaining her presence, "I need to be somewhere where people still have some values." It surprised me, I thought she was deeply committed to another church. I didn't ask what she meant, though, because of the other visitors. I wonder if Karl's warnings are making me paranoid?

I like to spend Sunday afternoons catching up with family and reading. All the while I was teaching I considered Sunday to be my day of rest, a legacy of my involvement in formal religion. I still enjoy having this rhythm to my week, and yesterday was a lovely autumn day. I took my book into the garden and read for an hour or more, then Judy saw her grandchildren off and came to join me. We talked and drank tea until dinner time. I felt a sort of calm all day. I knew an idea, or more, a way forward concerning the tent people, was fermenting in my mind, and I felt comfortable to let it brew.

And sure enough, today I have a clearer idea about what I want to do. From everything I've been told I think the encampment could be there for the winter. The Feeding Centre will stop them from starving, and will know what to do about other practical problems. I am concerned about the education of those children. My plan is to talk to a few people, see whether we can find somewhere to gather the kids together, and do our best to give them a minimum of education. I'm sure there will be all sorts of health and safety issues and insurance, and I can't imagine who might lend us a hall or room, but we've got to try. It seems like a really big idea, and a part of me wants to just stop now. I am retired, I have a pleasant life, and I can foresee all sorts of complications if I follow this route, but I think I have to. I have to 'do what love requires', as my community says. So I will take some time now, try to still my mind, and hold this venture in the Light. If it is right, it will work out.

Meanwhile I have a straightforward day ahead of me. I'm going in early to the shop, so that we can sort out the stuff that has come in over the last few days. There's a sort of irony that donations increase in direct relation to the number of evictions, which has been quite high recently. People are supposed to clear their houses before they leave, but I suppose they have nowhere to take all those unimportant things that seem to accumulate however tight money is. The Council workers who perform the evictions are supposed to sell anything left behind to help pay for the arrears of rent, and I have heard that they are not beyond taking some things for themselves, as perks of the job. However, most of the stuff is of no value and anyhow, sorting it is a huge job, so one way or another, it ends up with us.

The shop is the only place where I usually hear popular music. We have quite a lot of students who volunteer with us, and they don't seem to listen to anything else. We also sell music from around the world, and sometimes we put that on the sound system. Sorting donations is not a pleasant task – a lot of the clothes smell, and it seems sad to reject beaten up soft toys which once must have meant everything to a child, but it has to be done. Nevertheless, what with the music and the outrageous humour of one or two of the students, these sorting sessions can be fun. I'm behind the counter all afternoon, but I'll meet Jo for tea at the Italian coffee house afterwards. She has to collect one of hers from ballet at 5.30pm.

I need to clean the flat, too – my usual Monday job, and it's already 9.30am. I seem to have made a slow start today. This evening I need to think about who I should talk to next about this schooling idea for the tent people.

Tuesday 13th September

Yesterday didn't work out a bit as I'd intended. I cleaned the flat, making a really good job of the bathroom, and was just about to leave when the phone rang, and it was Karl. He said he had unexpectedly been given the afternoon off, and would I like to come over. I explained about the shop and tea with Jo, and he said, "Skip tea with Jo, I'll pick you up at 4.30 from the shop."

26

Of course I agreed. Why do I do this? I have a streak of wanting to please people, I know, but I don't think there's anyone else in the world who can make me change my plans just like that, because it pleases them. When I first knew Karl it was a different matter. I was bowled over by him, he was so unlike all my other friends and so fascinating. But now … A part of me thinks he really has been given the afternoon off unexpectedly, but another part of me thinks that it was always a day off, that he was meeting some woman somewhere but their plans have fallen through, so he has phoned me. Anyhow, I texted Jo, changed into my best jeans, and put a little eye make-up on, before I headed off for the shop.

Karl seemed to be in a good mood. There isn't really a parking place outside the shop but his car has an ATTF number plate so nobody is going to question him. He came in around 4.15pm, said, "Hi," to me very casually, and started looking around the shop. I didn't want to go early. I think it's unfair on the other helpers to be left to do all the end of the day work on their own, but Karl has this way of looking impatient which makes me feel pressured. The student who was working with me must have picked it up too, because she said "You go on, I can manage here," so I gathered up my bag and jacket, and left.

Karl hardly ever talks when he's driving, except to comment on other people's skills behind the wheel. I know he is an Advanced Driver, I think it might be part of his job. Yesterday, though, he seemed quite light hearted. It had been raining earlier but the sun was out, and he was humming under his breath – rather tunelessly. As we left the main road going up the hill Karl said, out of the blue, "There's another one."

"Another what?" I asked. I had been thinking that I would need to apologise to Jo this afternoon when we knit, for just dropping her like that.

"Another house for rent, the third one in this road."

I saw what he meant. The houses there are semi-detached with front and rear gardens, good places to raise families, and three had 'For Rent' signs in the driveways, all put up by the same estate agent.

"I think it's rent inflation," I said. "You know, now that the law has been changed landlords are putting up the rent and tenants are having to leave." I thought about the people in the park.

"Market forces," said Karl, and I couldn't tell whether he approved of what was happening or not. "Our foreign cousins can pay much more than our people, and they like to live in this area. Good transport to London. Good schools."

We had meatballs in a very hot sauce for dinner, with rice and cabbage. It doesn't sound amazing, but it was, as was the fresh fruit salad. Karl went through a phase of making his own ice cream but today we had bought stuff, very expensive and probably very fattening! Afterwards we watched the second half of the Chile football match, then channel-hopped until we found a satirical comedy, which I rather like.

A few minutes into it there was one of those questions about who is the odd man out. I, of course, did not recognise three of the celebrities involved, but Karl said at once, "Eviction! The chancellor is the odd one!"

He was right. It seems that one picture was of a football manager who had lost his job two games into the season after a vote of no confidence from the shareholders, one picture showed a drummer who had been dropped from a group because he could not get a visa for their American tour, one picture was the Chancellor of the Exchequer (the only one I recognised) who had survived a cabinet reshuffle, and one picture was of a random member of the public, evicted from his home following the changes in the rent law, which is still big news.

We both laughed because the way the quiz master explained it all, it sounded really funny, especially the bit about the drummer, but then Karl said, "Do you know there are people camping on the park near you?"

"Yes," I said. "Of course I do. It was in the paper." Why didn't I say I had been over and talked to them? I suppose because I knew he wouldn't approve.

He didn't say anything else for a moment and I thought that was it. The quiz master was recounting a story about a crazy Russian diplomat. Then Karl said, "There's going to be trouble of course. Eventually." Then he added, "It's best to stay away you know." He didn't look at me, it was almost as if he were talking to himself, but I felt uncomfortable. Was it just that Karl can read me so well? And why does he always think he knows best?

The phone rang just as we were sorting out my sofa bed. Quite often when I'm there Karl doesn't answer the phone, just lets the answer machine pick it up, but he checked the number, said, "Excuse me," to me, and took the call. It wasn't much of a conversation, just, "Yes, sure. No. Right. Nine o'clock. I'll be there."

When he put the phone down he said, "I'll take you home quite early tomorrow morning. That was work."

When I went to the bathroom I saw in through the open door of his bedroom. His khaki jacket was on the back of his chair and his shiny black shoes were lined up next to each other. The shoulder tabs on the jacket looked different – there was a four pointed star and a crown, in red. Was that what I had seen before? There was no point in asking. The ATTF is not the sort of organisation where people talk about these things, and nobody in my family has had anything to do with the military – if the ATTF is counted as military – so I have no way of guessing.

I showered when I got in this morning and put on clean clothes, but I still feel grimy. It obviously can't be the result of sorting donations yesterday afternoon, so what is it? I know I was not really open with Karl, and I wonder if he was not really straight with me either. Our community believes strongly in integrity and speaking Truth, and I feel I did not talk honestly with Karl about the tents in the park and about my involvement. Yet something makes me feel I don't want to talk to him about it all. I feel a lack of ease, but I have just sat for ten minutes looking out at the garden, trying to settle my spirit, and I have got nowhere. I do not know how to break through this mood, which is like a barrier to the Light within me.

Well, I am back earlier than I expected and even after writing this journal, I have lots of time at my disposal this morning. I don't need to go out, but I usually make a point of doing something physical every day, for the exercise. The closest good walk is round the park, but I am reluctant to go there until I know what my plans are, so I think I will go down to the recreation centre in the other direction, look at the little art gallery there, and have a coffee. Fran and Jo will be here soon after 2.00pm, and I want to watch the documentary about the Red Crescent this evening.

Wednesday 14th September

I want always to be honest with myself, that is part of the point of this journal. Right, so can I work out what is bothering me? I slept badly last night and woke at dawn. I made a coffee and sat by the French windows as colour gradually came back into the world. It had been raining in the night but by now it had stopped, and each time a gust of wind blew through the trees the rain scattered from the leaves. I went back to bed after my coffee and lay there listening to the radio news until I dozed off again. I had one of those half-awake, half-asleep dreams. I had arranged to meet someone at the gallery coffee shop but he did not come. I was wearing my tartan pyjamas. In my dream it was sometimes my father and sometimes Karl who I was hoping to see. I woke up feeling sluggish and demoralised, my mind more than half still in my dream rather than in my real life.

I think it is to do with Jo's reaction when I apologised to her for not meeting her for tea on Monday. "No problem," she assured me, but she was looking out of my kitchen window, not at me. "I went to Marco's anyhow and Sky was there, talking to that tall guy from the Centre. Sky asked after you, she wanted to know whether we had discussed the tent dwellers in the park. She seemed to think you have some idea for helping. I told her you were with Karl. I don't think she was very impressed."

I don't like to talk to Sky about Karl. I know perfectly well that she doesn't like anyone who imposes the wearing of a uniform, or who chooses to wear one. She told me so once. She even includes school uniforms. She said that anyone who wants first to make everyone look alike by dressing them in identical clothes, and then to introduce new distinctions between them with stripes or badges, has deep psychological problems. He or she needs to iron out the creases of reality and to impose some sort of simplistic order onto something, the human race, which is endlessly complicated. A healthy person, Sky thinks, can at least deal with, and probably enjoy, the endless differences between people.

It bothers me that so many of my friends probably don't approve of Karl, or anyhow, of my friendship with him. Jo didn't say so, but she must have thought it rather impolite of me, at least, to have cancelled tea like that, and I suspect that at Meeting some people just cannot understand how I can be comfortable socialising with someone who stands for the sort of activities linked with the ATTF. I suppose I would be quite surprised myself, except that each stage in our relationship seemed to happen quite naturally, and now here I am. It is like walking in Scotland. You are hiking across pleasant, springy turf talking to your companions, keeping your eyes on the path already visible on the next slope, a few reeds are growing here and there and lots of wild flowers, then suddenly you put your foot down and it sinks deep into black mire. You find you are in the middle of a bog, and none of you know how you got there.

I was going through a stage of lacking in confidence when I first met Karl. When I was young I had been very sure of myself, particularly in my working life, and so I had been happy despite the long hours. The job suited my idealistic streak too. I felt that despite our political masters we were creating a new and more just education system, a system where children from the least privileged backgrounds would be able to achieve. Ways of examining pupils were being changed, we had to keep attending courses and often we had to create our own materials because the production of new text books couldn't keep up with the endless adjustments. Like a lot of us back in those days, I felt as if my voice could be heard, not by those in power but by my pupils and their parents.

Things changed some time in the second decade of my teaching career. The government wanted to stop the sorts of initiatives I had been involved in, so they needed to convince the public that the schools and the teachers were doing a bad job. As the Right got stronger we had less and less freedom, until it got to the stage where we had almost no personal input into our own lessons. We taught what we were told to teach, in the order and manner in which we were told to teach it. Even then, we couldn't be sure of the outcomes. Goal posts were changed randomly. I could teach something one way one year and my kids would do well, I could teach a similar group of students in exactly the same way the following year, and they would do badly. All but the most gullible of us knew it was all to score political points, but it left me feeling helpless.

Some teachers adjusted and lots of teachers left, of course. Some had bad inspection reports, some started to teach the increasing number of kids excluded from main stream schools, and several of my closest friends went abroad. They were replaced by a different sort of person, less idealistic, seemingly motivated by the desire for promotion and for status. Good capitalists, in fact. My politics couldn't be hidden because of the things I was known to do out of school, especially after the demonstrations against the New Alliance. It was also at about this time that I departed from mainstream religion, like everything else in my world it seemed to be moving to the right without me. By the time Karl came on the scene I was feeling a bit like a creature washed up on an alien shore.

After the incident when Karl came in for the records of those Year 10 kids, I didn't expect ever to see him again. Beyond a passing reflection, that I wouldn't have expected an ATTF officer to be like him, I probably didn't give him another thought. I suspect I didn't even know his name, and his rank will have meant nothing to me.

Then, one hot afternoon a few days later, I was sitting in my office at the end of the day typing letters, with two detainees sitting outside doing their overdue homework, when my phone rang.

"Hi there," greeted the cheerful receptionist, "your four o'clock appointment is here."

I flicked to the diary page on my DeV21 and looked at it in surprise. I hadn't noted down a four o'clock meeting, and I'm usually pretty good at keeping my appointments up to date. I looked a week ahead, in case I had just put it in the wrong slot, but that wasn't possible, I had a departmental workshop from 3.30 to 4.30 that week.

Feeling a bit worried I set my papers to one side, minimised the page on the screen, and headed down the corridor. I really don't like having meetings for which I'm not prepared. I felt I had been caught off balance. My immediate problem was that the parent (it probably was a parent) would expect me to know who she or he was, and I would probably have no clue.

Then, at Reception, there stood Karl, in uniform but without his jacket or tie. He was looking at the pottery on display in the cabinets.

"Good afternoon," he said formally, "I hope I'm not taking you away from something urgent. Do you think we could have a brief talk?"

The receptionist had her head down, but the earpieces she wore when dealing with phone calls were round her neck. I knew she was listening, wondering what my business might be with the ATTF.

"Of course," I said, "no problem. Come this way."

Karl looked at the receptionist, back at me, and to my great surprise, winked at me. Then he said, still in a formal voice, "I hope you will be able to help me."

The kids outside my office were messing around. One was out of his place and they both had their own DeVs on their tables. When they saw Karl they scuttled, there is no other word for it, so that by the time we had walked along the corridor to my door they were sitting up straight, work tablets open on pages which looked like maths, and heads down.

"Take a seat," I said, as I closed the door. "How can I help?"

Karl sat in the arm chair by the window, leaned back and crossed his legs, and said in a matter-of-fact voice, "You could have dinner with me."

Now, I used to read romantic novels when I was a teenager. Who didn't? But since then I have had little time for overtures like this, and little experience of them, too. When I have had relationships with people they have generally been as the result of working together or belonging to the same organisations. I remember feeling as if this were like a film script.

I must have looked as surprised as I felt. "You haven't got any meetings this evening," Karl pointed out, then, slightly sheepishly, "You keep your diary on your DeV."

Afterwards I realised that his comment suggested he had accessed my pages, and that he could already know a huge amount about me, but just at that minute all I was thinking was that the walls of our offices were thin and the kids working outside – if they were working – could in all likelihood hear everything.

I probably said something silly, I can't remember now. I'm sure I went red. Karl was in complete control. He just stood up, said quite loudly in his formal voice, "Thank you for your help. An hour from now would be convenient. I will pick you up from here." Then, as he opened the office door he turned, shook hands with me and said, "You have been very helpful. Thank you for your cooperation. I can find my own way out."

The kids, like the receptionist, had their heads down, and like the receptionist, I knew they were not concentrating on the work in front of them. I guessed that they might go home and tell their parents and their friends that an ATTF officer had been to see me, and Karl had made it clear as he left that I was not in trouble. It is, in my opinion, a sad reflection on our society that some parents would have thought more highly of me, hearing that. The fact that in the months to come Karl picked me up from school in his ATTF registered car and sometimes in uniform, is probably the biggest reason, and maybe the only reason, that I was able to keep my job until retirement. But even then, it was not easy.

I was not just demoralised at work at the time that I met Karl. I was in a real muddle about religion. I had moved away from the church where I had been at home for years because of what I thought of as their illiberal attitudes, but I was not really settled where I am now, I was more like a squatter. I had those strict moral principles left over from my previous existence, but I no longer knew why I held on to them. I was lonely, I suppose, and ready for Karl to sweep me off my feet.

Afterwards I realised that Karl had courtship – or was it seduction? – down to a fine art. He didn't rush me. He was kind. We had a whole lot of fun, and he also listened sympathetically to all my woes about work. We had one big argument about religion but then rarely touched on the subject again. One of the things I loved about Karl in those days was that he didn't seem ever to try to change my mind about things. It was clear that he thought I was naïve, naïve about politics and naïve about religion, but he seemed happy to accept that, he even seemed to find it attractive in me, although even in those days I knew that sometimes he was trying to warn me. Mostly he seemed to warn me not to trust people. I stopped keeping my personal diary on my DeV and just put my professional engagements there, and I was probably a bit more circumspect about what I said in the classroom or in staff meetings. When I started to write to Simon this caution paid dividends. I never make political or idealistic comments to him, knowing that although most of our letters are hand written, they can be read by the censors.

I was never quite comfortable about my relationship with Karl, though. Partly I thought it was my discarded but not forgotten sexual morality. Hauntings, after all, are always a product of the past. Another part of me thought it was more complicated. For one thing, it was clear that Karl and I were diametrically opposed on matters of politics and human rights, even on matters of honesty. Karl had accessed my private DeV pages, once we knew each other and were involved together he didn't even try to hide it. He also told me quite openly that when Pat was questioning my judgement over Tom Fox, who the school wanted to exclude and who I thought we should keep, he had forged several emails purporting to be from parents in support of me, and he had changed Pat's professional profile rating from A to B. The result for me was good. It was good for Tom too, who stayed and passed most of his exams, and Tom's parents were incredibly grateful. I think Pat knew that something underhand had happened, even if she didn't know how, and I think Senior Management looked at me a bit askance after that too. Pat was, after all, their protégée and I was considered to be rather a difficult member of staff.

I was grateful for Karl's intervention, although he only told me about it afterwards, when the Head had told me that Tom could, after all, stay at school, and that there would be no further disciplinary action against me. Still, another part of me felt it was wrong. It is Truth that is powerful, and a part of me would rather have lost honestly than have won through Karl's less than honest assistance. To my shame, I didn't even try to explain that to Karl. He would have thought I was being childish or unreasonable; after all, he had done something for Tom through his subterfuge which I was incapable of achieving through honest means, and anyhow, what was the point of me behaving honestly when Pat had been using her status to win points?

Perhaps 'shame' sums up the lurking feelings I had then, and which I recorded yesterday morning too, and it is that same feeling which my dream brought into my consciousness again today.

All along I suspected that Karl's commitment to me was less than my commitment to him. Another residue of my youth was a sense that you don't get involved with someone unless it is 'serious'. Part of me wanted my relationship with Karl to be serious, but only ever one part of me. As I settled very gradually into my new worshipping community and became free to leave behind many of my earlier, rather restricting beliefs, I felt more and more strongly about those values with which I was left. I knew I could not live with a man whose career choices had taken him into the ATTF.

But if I'm feeling shame now, sitting in front of my balcony windows, it can't be because of my relationship with Karl. We stopped being a pair several years ago. In fact, I rather suspect that from Karl's point of view we never really were. So what gives me this slight feeling of sickness now, this discomfort? I feel I'm involved in a betrayal, but I'm not sure who is being betrayed.

There's a weariness attached to this sense of shame too, because even as I know I should open my inner understanding to Truth, to find how to deal with my concerns, I also know that I've been here many times before. I was here yesterday morning. There's little point in asking for guidance if I don't have the stamina to see it through. As often as I consider breaking off all contact with Karl, I more or less know I will not do it. I suppose this is what it is like to be an addict.

I will sit here in silence for a while, and ask for strength.

Oh dear – now I realise that I have spent all morning writing this journal, and in less than an hour I'll need to leave for Meeting. This seems to me to sum up the Karl problem: I have been sitting here all morning thinking about him when I should have been thinking about the tent people, and about the discussion we had yesterday afternoon. I wish I were involved with someone whose influence was to make me think about others, instead of endlessly analysing myself.

Thursday 15th September

It is just after 6.00am and still dark. I'm resisting turning on the heating, although there's no logic to that. This building produces and stores its own electricity and I do no damage to the environment or my bank account if I turn the heating on. I just don't want to admit that winter is on the way.

I slept well last night and I have woken feeling full of purpose and hope. Yesterday started badly but it turned out to be a really good day. Meeting for Worship was lovely. There were the usual people, plus one of the counsellors who has started to hire the small room at the back, and who is taking quite an interest in our activities. I arrived feeling out of sorts. I felt I had wasted the morning going over thoughts about Karl which I must have expressed in almost the same words several times in my journal over the last few years, and my spirits were still heavy from that dream, and from sleeping after breakfast. I felt scruffy too. My hair felt messy and I was wearing jeans with turn-ups which, I sometimes think, might look silly on a woman my age. Anyhow, I settled down to worship and tried to clear my mind.

Perhaps it helped that yesterday I had no pride or self confidence. I came as I am, weak, easily deflected from the life I ought to lead, aware of my need, of not having anything to offer. Very quickly that special sort of stillness descended on the meeting. It is difficult to describe the way it feels. When we were children we used to go on holiday on the north Norfolk coast. There are some beautiful open, unspoilt beaches there, very flat and sandy. The tides go in and out for miles, and sometimes we would be playing on the wet sand when suddenly the sea would flood in. There would be no waves, just water rushing silently in over our sandcastles and sand boats and mazes. So it is, sometimes, in Meeting. I consciously brought my failing self to the Truth, and then that power of calm, of peace, of wholeness, came flooding in. It smoothed my spirit as the tide would smooth away our sand-works. This is a thing too deep for words. Even pictures and images can't do it justice. I rested in the health of it, and felt myself restored.

Later, when we had shaken hands and listened to notices, we went through for lunch, and there was a quiet sense of unity among us all. We talked less than usual and smiled more, and Jill, the counsellor, said as she took her place at the table, "I should come to Meeting more often ... I had no idea ..."

Afterwards I did a little bit of shopping (milk and eggs), worked a couple of hours in the shop, and bought some odd balls of wool at the market on my way home. The calmness stayed deep inside me. Bearing Karl's warnings in mind, I mapped out the ideas for the tent people's school in a notebook rather than on my DeV, the plan Jo, Fran, Sabina and I had made on Tuesday.

I realise that Wednesday morning was difficult and I didn't note down our conversation over knitting on Tuesday. This journal is only for me, so is there any point in telling myself what I already know we said? Yes, I think so. My journal is only for my eyes, but it is for my eyes in the future as well as in the present. There may come a time when I want to look back over exactly what happened. Our community has always seen the value of keeping records.

Jo had arrived first and had mentioned the conversation with Sky, which I noted yesterday. Sabina brought her baby again, and Fran arrived with home made biscuits. We sat in my living room and listened to a beautiful CD of Arab music which I had bought at the shop. Jo had mentioned the tent people before the others arrived, but it was Sabina who raised the topic again and I was glad she did, because I had no idea what her attitude to such issues might have been.

"My grandmother taught me to knit," she said, "she said we should learn all the survival skills we can, because we never know what life might bring." She peered over at the baby, who was asleep in her Moses basket. "My grandmother came here not knowing a word of English, to marry a man she had only met once. It was against the law, of course, but people do what they have to do."

"Was she happy?" Fran was knitting a striped red and green square, with the stripes going diagonally across because she always starts from the corner.

"Oh, I think so," Sabina was thoughtful. "My grandpa was a lovely man, and successful. My grandmother would never have had such a good life back home, and I don't think she would have been so well respected. She was lucky." She paused for a moment. "Not everyone is."

We generally agreed, muttering our yeses.

After a few more minutes Sabina spoke again. "It was lovely yesterday afternoon. I took Yasmin for a walk in the park. Have you seen the tent people there?"

"They've been camping there for several weeks," Jo said. "I think there are more every day."

Fran said, "It breaks my heart. There are children and an old man. I never thought our country would come to this."

"We could do something, maybe?" Sabina was tentative. "I know you are good people, and we are taught 'the key of paradise is to love the poor and the destitute'. I'm shy to go over there on my own, but I'd like to help them." She blushed a little. "Imran says we can afford it."

Jo looked at me. I said, "I have been thinking we might start a sort of school for them. There are no places for them at St. Mark's or Peeble's Way. I talked to a friend about it last Saturday. But I don't really know where to go from here. We would need somewhere to meet, and there are bound to be loads of rules and regulations. Do you remember when the government wanted parents to start their own schools? Only the middle classes ever managed it, and most of those schools failed or became mainstream within ten years."

"When I was little," said Sabina, "my cousins and I used to all go to my grandmother's every afternoon. She taught us all sorts of things – reading and writing, knitting and cooking, and she told us stories…"

"I don't think the families in the park have grandparents like that," commented Fran.

"No – but you see, my grandmother wasn't a teacher. She wasn't even a child minder. She was just our grandmother. But it didn't stop us from learning from her."

I was thinking hard. "But I think there might be different rules for families," I said. "If kids started coming to this flat and we started teaching them, I think the authorities would close us down." I thought a bit more about it. "Some of the neighbours wouldn't like it either."

"What if we went there?" suggested Jo. "Do you think there are any laws about visiting friends and teaching their children something while you're there?"

We all looked at each other. Fran had a frown, Jo looked thoughtful and Sabina was grinning. "It's worth a try, isn't it?" she said.

It is light now. I want to spend some quiet time holding that conversation, so to speak, in my open hands, asking for that tide of wholeness to wash over it. 'Unless the Lord builds the house, the labourers labour in vain'. Then, if it still feels as right as it feels now,

I will walk over to the tent people and see if there's someone with whom I can discuss it all. Then I'll see how my day works out.

Friday 16th September

It's really tempting to send emails to Jo, Fran and Sabina, telling them about yesterday, but it's silly to run risks, and I have to think about them as well as me. It's just that, although I'm trying to stay calm and focussed, the way those elderly Peace Workers were when I first went to Meeting and we were preparing for the demonstrations against the New Alliance, the fact is that I'm pretty excited.

I didn't want to go across the park too early, so I caught up with my ironing first, had a coffee and looked at a charity catalogue that had come through the door. At about this time I usually start thinking about Christmas, although I rarely buy anything until the end of October. I left the flat around 10.00am and followed my usual circuit round the park.

There were indeed more tents, and also a sort of hut made out of bits of wood and some rusty corrugated iron. The campers have kept to the very edge of the park, the new dwellings are in amongst the trees where they are less obvious from a distance. Some wheelie bins have appeared with hand written notices on them, 'Glass', 'Recycling – please wash first' and 'compost'. The ground is badly trodden down and muddy, and there's a bare patch of earth where there must have been a fire. I looked for the girl I had spoken to last time, but at first I couldn't work out which was her tent. It looked different because of the extra tents beyond it.

The little boy was playing with another child in the woods. I saw him before I saw his mother, who was sitting on a log watching. I went over to her.

"Hi," I said. "How's it going?"

She had seen me coming and didn't look surprised. "Fine," she said, "good. He already knows the letter 'J' for his name, and 'M' for 'mummy'."

"That's great." I really was pleased. "And how are you? Any news from the housing people?"

She shrugged and looked away. "We won't hear from them," she said. "None of us will. They don't plan to rehouse anyone else." She stared across at the children playing, and called out, "Don't go too near to the river!" Then she added, "We're getting ourselves organised. We're going to be a sort of cooperative, all contributing what we can. It could work." She sighed. "But I'm dreading the winter."

I sat down next to her, and she moved along a little to give me a more comfortable piece of log. "I ... some friends and I have had an idea," I said.

She looked sharply at me. "Yes?" Her suspicion was loud and clear.

I ploughed on. "Your Jamie, and the other children ... I used to be a teacher. Would you like it if ... I mean, would it help if we came over now and again to teach them? Just a few of us?"

The girl looked away, down at her feet, and kicked the dead bark on the ground. "That's kind," she said, then looked up at me. "Really kind. We couldn't pay you."

"Of course not, no." I was a little shocked at the very thought.

"I'll have to talk to the others," she said. "How would it work?"

She's called Claire. Her husband's called Gordon and Jamie's little friend, playing in the woods, is Sophie. There are seven children there at present, all denied school places. Last night they will have discussed our proposition, and this evening I'll go over and hear their decision. I'm at the shop this afternoon, from 1.00pm until 4.00pm, and if I get a minute I plan to look again at the second-hand books. I'll do my grocery shopping as I always do on Fridays. Perhaps I'll buy chocolate biscuits for the children.

Saturday 17th September

It's pouring with rain. The ventilator window in the kitchen is open, and I can hear a mixture of different noises, like a sort of orchestra, the gurgle of the water in the gutters, the gentle chatter of the rain on the leaves, the swish of occasional cars in the road behind the flats, and sometimes a pattering against the window when the wind blows. There are some gentle indoor noises too, all predictable and in their ways as soothing as the sound of rain. I can hear my fridge purring in the kitchen. Every now and again my phone makes that little 'beep' that tells me it is logging in, and sometimes I hear a hum from the lift, which rises and falls between my kitchen and the bathroom wall of the flat next door. The rain makes the air smell different, of autumn and of earth, even though I'm on the first floor. I slept deeply and well last night and woke around seven. I've had my breakfast and cleaned up the kitchen. My day stretches ahead in a contented and satisfactory way.

I'm glad Jo texted me so cautiously, although I think that all this caution about electronic communication is probably overdone. Fran, Sabina, Jo and I are hardly a threat to the safety of the nation, and while a lot of people might be suspicious about the motives of those of us who question as much as we do, it seems clear that a lot of other people sympathise with the sorts of opinions we have. I can't believe that anyone would seriously consider us a security risk. It was different at school; teachers have to be authority figures, in effect we were influencing kids on behalf of the state who pays us, but the country is full of voluntary sector workers, human rights groups and those religious organisations which have not moved to the right, and any surveillance team would be hard pressed to keep tabs on us all. Nevertheless Jo's innocuous message, suggesting we have coffee while her daughter is fitted for her ballet outfit, would surely seem totally innocent to anyone listening in, and I really want to talk to her about yesterday.

It was such a good evening. I walked over to the park after dinner, Claire had said most of the men would be back by then, and it would be dusk, I would be less obvious. I took the biscuits and wore my old jacket, I didn't want to seem too well off to the people I was going to meet.

The guy who I later found was called Alfred came to meet me, and we walked towards the camp fire while he explained what Claire had already told me, that they were trying to work together to do what they could to look after each other. "We've had to be a bit harsh," he said, "a group of street sleepers came over yesterday evening, just kids really, but they were high as kites. We've got children here, and we're not … we aren't your typical rough sleepers. If we let them join us they'd just be trouble." He paused, then said more quietly, as we reached the camp fire, "I used to volunteer at a night shelter when I was a student. I never thought I'd be in this mess."

They had lit the camp fire and quite a crowd of people was sitting around it. Someone has found some old car seats and an arm chair has appeared from somewhere, everyone else was sitting on ground on bits of plastic, or were perched on two lengths of tree trunk pulled out from the woods. Claire was sitting with Jamie on her lap, rocking him gently back and forth. A tall, skinny man – more of a boy, really, was squatting next to them, chewing and staring into the fire. Gordon, I suppose.

Alfred introduced me and briefly explained our idea. "We've got to hope they'll let the kids into school soon," he said, a little desperately, I thought, "but until then any education is better than none."

An older man was squinting across the fire at me, his face suspicious. "So what's in it for you?" he wanted to know, "Just asking."

I swallowed. "Well…" Then I thought, honesty is always the best policy. "I think it's all wrong," I said. "The rent act, people being evicted, the cuts, the sheer selfishness of the system now. I don't want to live in a country where this sort of thing happens. I've seen it – somewhere else – and I just want to help. All four of us do."

The tent people were quiet. Alfred said, "Wish there were more like you."

"There might be," I said, putting all my cards on the table, so to speak. "I'm a member of a group – Jo and Fran too – and we want to try to get their backing. If you're happy for us to do that?"

"What group? Where?" The tent people were wary, I couldn't blame them. "What could they do that you and your friends can't do alone?"

I explained about our community, how we have grown to nearly two hundred locally in the last few years after some churches came out so strongly for the New Alliance and our resulting heavy engagement in military activity in the Caribbean, how cautious we have become since others around the country have become subject to harassment, or have even been arrested. "When we started in the seventeenth century we were badly persecuted and a central committee was called 'Meeting for Affliction'. There was a lot of talk around the turn of this century about changing the name. We'd become a small, quite wealthy middle-class organisation and our members generally didn't suffer much affliction at all, probably less than the average Brit, except perhaps for the peace activists. But we're starting to suffer now. Our Business Meetings are entirely closed, if we discuss this idea there I don't think anyone else will find out."

By now the light was fading fast. A woman with rat's tail hair and a bandanna round her neck said, "How do we know you're a teacher?" Then, to the others, "Could be a child abuser for all we know."

People moved uncomfortably in their seats. The woman was right.

Claire spoke up. "One of us will have to be there all the time. It's the only way."

Her husband added, "I don't think we can ask the police to do disclosure and barring service checks."

"Where will you do it, run this school?"

"How often?"

"Where will you get books and stuff?"

So I explained our ideas and passed the biscuits round, and someone poured some hot, dark tea into a strange assortment of mugs and cups, and we discussed the whole thing further.

"Doesn't sound like much of a school," said the older man. "When you think what proper schools do."

"We can't have a proper school," Alfred pointed out. "They're making things as hard as they dare for us. If they let us have a school, or even simple things like piped water, people would say that they were encouraging us. They're hoping that when winter comes we'll move away. That's what they want. It's happening all round the country, they close feeding centres, they put these daft restrictions on night shelters and drop-in centres, and they forbid people to take soup to the rough sleepers at night."

I could hear disgruntled agreement. Claire's husband turned to me. "What about you? They won't like you doing this, you know. There could be trouble where you work."

"I'm retired," I grinned. "Untouchable."

"And the others?"

"Jo and Sabina are stay-at-home mothers, Fran works part time for the Red Cross and helps with a youth club. I think we should be safe enough. And to be honest, what could they do?"

"You'd be surprised," said Alfred, under his breath.

My plan for today is therefore to see Jo and catch her up with everything, then to come back here and think through a programme of study. That sounds a bit grand, but if we're going to work together then we need to agree the order we are going to teach things. Then I need to write a report for Meeting. We do our business on the first Sunday of the month and I expect a real grilling over this. We are nothing if not thorough.

I really want to surf around a bit to find out what is happening with the homeless in other towns, but any internet research can be traced. I'll look at fair trade sites for Christmas gifts instead. I commit this day, with joy, to the Light.

CHAPTER 2

Monday 4ᵗʰ October

I am still in my pyjamas, sitting by the French windows where the underfloor heating is doing its 'smart' thing, and sensing where I am. My feet are toasty warm and I feel good. It started to get light forty minutes or so ago, with that grey-flat sort of lightness which precedes sunrise, but now the sun is up, casting long dappled green and gold patterns on the lawn, which come and go as the clouds scud across the sky. I decided to write this journal before I do anything else, because I woke up feeling so thankful, and so certain that we are doing the right thing.

I thought the Business Meeting yesterday would be difficult, and in a way I was right. Jo and Fran were there, although Jo had to leave at one point to sort out her daughter, who was in the children's room, and I feared she might miss the crucial discussion. It wasn't really a discussion, of course, that isn't how we do things. The clerk said a few words about our agenda item and then asked me to speak, and afterwards anyone was free to ask questions or contribute thoughts or ideas, if they felt Truth required it of them.

I explained about the tent people and about the regular contact we three and Sabina now have with them. I outlined the sorts of things we would like to teach: basic literacy and numeracy, creative activities, any other areas of knowledge for which we could find resources, and anything the children seemed to want to follow up. Good practice says we keep these introductory explanations brief. I sat down with my heart pounding, fearful that too much cold water would be poured on our ideas.

47

There was the usual silence – nothing is supposed to be hurried in these Business Meetings – then a lovely elderly man rose creakily and coughed. "I hope," he said, "that we can lend all our support to this venture." He sat again.

Another silence. Zoe stood, looking worried. "I haven't spoken to the tent people but I understand that theirs is not a legal encampment. If we involve ourselves with them in this way, are we not supporting law breaking? There are many legitimate, government approved schemes into which we can pour our energies. We know how Friends are being challenged across the country for our stance to the rent act and to the new restrictions on health and social care. Perhaps we should consider whether we might achieve more and bring less trouble upon ourselves by working within existing organisations – perhaps at the Feeding Centre?"

This was what I feared. I wanted to jump up and reply, but it was not my place to say anything more unless asked. This was a time for the Spirit to guide us into Truth, not for me to win an argument. Oh, but I wanted to win the argument! I closed my eyes and tried to pray, "Thy will be done."

There was another movement behind me as Fran stood. "The Feeding Centre is doing a good thing," she remarked, "but they can't educate children. I hold that basic literacy is the right of every human being." She sat again.

More silence. A cough. Two people whispered at the back. I tried to pray. I tried not to feel angry with Zoe.

Elizabeth, who is as old as the hills and almost as wise, gripped her stick and rose unsteadily to her feet. "On Thursday my fifth great grandchild was born." She smiled across at Maya, they have known each other for half a lifetime. "Peter's second," she clarified. "I don't know what the coming years will bring for little Angelica, and I don't expect to be here to see it. But I do know that we are asked, 'Are you following Jesus' example of love in action?' I believe that if the people around our little Angelica are trying to follow Jesus' example of love in action then she will be all right. I think this venture could be Jesus' love in action for the children in the tents. We should think carefully, Friends, in case in our fear or caution we answer 'no' to that query instead of 'yes'."

I thought I felt the mood change. There was a deeper stillness. The clerk looked slowly around the room, one eyebrow raised.

Johnny rose from his seat near the door. "I could help by teaching some basic science," he offered, "if we could do evening classes. And Maria knows about macramé."

"We have piles of books in the attic," Andy said, speaking as he stood.

"I hope," Sean said, leaning forward in his wheelchair, "that we would not let the fear of opposition or unpopularity deafen us to the Spirit."

There was another silence. "Friends," the clerk addressed the meeting again. "I think we have found a way forward." He turned to me. "Will you feel able to report back in November to let us know how you are getting on?" Then to everyone, "If you feel you wish to be involved in this, please make sure that you have made clear what you have to offer. And Friends – maybe we need to be a bit circumspect about what we say about this, outside our Meetings for Business?"

I walked through the nature reserve and visited the camp via the broken footbridge at the back. There was hardly anyone around, but Alfred was sitting under a tree with a dog at his heels, reading a Saturday paper. He was pleased with my news. Then I went home to my quiet Sunday afternoon and my busy thoughts.

It is a lovely morning now. I'll clean the flat this morning and work at the shop this afternoon. Before I go, I think I'll print out the lesson scheme we decided on last Tuesday. I haven't seen Amy for a while, so maybe I'll email her too. Lunch some time this week would be good, if she's free. I have that energetic, positive feeling which I associate with being in the right place at the right time. Before I do anything I think I will settle my heart in the Truth, with thanksgiving.

The post yesterday brought a horrible shock to me, and I feel sick and on edge, unable to concentrate on anything. They have given Simon an execution date early in January. First I got Simon's letter, saying he thought it was about to happen, then I turned on my emails and there was the confirmation. Of course I always knew this was a possibility. In fact, as the years have passed and Simon's last appeals have been unsuccessful, I have known that in theory it was inevitable. But knowing is one thing, really realising it is another.

It seems impossible to believe. Simon is a quiet man with sleepy-looking brown eyes and black hair, so straight that he must have white or Native American genes in him somewhere. He is a practical man, the sort of person who fixed his own car and helped his father build a back porch, before he was arrested. He's the sort of person who would be good to have as a neighbour, because you could ask him for help without feeling you were intruding. He told me once about putting up storm shutters all along their street when they thought a hurricane was coming. It seems crazy that a man like Simon, healthy, friendly, kind, generous, should be alive at Christmas, alive for the new year, then just killed, in cold blood, early in January. My mind can't accept it, but somewhere in the pit of my stomach I know it's true. I must have woken up a dozen times last night and now I feel tense and jittery, the way I used to feel on the morning of a performance management observation in the last few years, when I felt they were only looking for my weaknesses.

I am not sure how to handle it. I know I should sit and wait in the Light, asking for peace and wholeness to come into my spirit, but I feel like walking around, like doing something with great energy. I almost wish I hadn't cleaned the flat yesterday, some good hearty polishing would suit my mood better than sitting in silence bringing the whole of my life under the ordering of the Spirit. I think of those older, more spiritual people I know, and I wonder what they would do? I can't imagine they would be thrown, as I am, by something I knew all along was part of the path I have chosen to walk.

The shame of it is that this afternoon we will have our last meeting, over the knitting, before we start our tent school tomorrow. This should be a time of excitement, of moving forward, the beginning of the fulfilment of a minor dream. Right now it just seems too much. Before, when I was in mainstream religion, people used to put things down to spiritual attack. The belief was that the forces of evil are everywhere, trying to oppose God and His people. Their explanation for this news about Simon, coming today, would be (I think) that we were being attacked by evil forces because the school is a project directed by God. One part of me, having been immersed in that way of thinking for half my life, is inclined to think even now that such an explanation is not unreasonable. Yet if I am honest with myself I really don't think the experiences of my existence can be unravelled in such a simple, fairy-story sort of way. I thought it was right – no, I felt guided – to write to Simon. I felt guided to start the tent school, and that guidance has been confirmed first by Jo and Fran – and, I suppose by Sabina – and now by Meeting. Sooner or later both commitments were bound to bring pressures into my life at the same time. It's part of being human to feel these stresses. It's part of being spiritual to let them help me to grow instead of damaging me. Perhaps it's part of my growth to be disciplined, to accept the sense of foreboding in my spirit and to do what love requires of me today, regardless of how I feel.

I will not ask for peace this morning. I will sit in silence and ask for strength, and for self discipline. Peace is a gift. Living in the Light is a command.

Wednesday 6th October

The jittery feeling is still there, but I think the time of silence did help, and I wrote a quick card to Simon afterwards. I doubt if many people yesterday will have guessed what big things are going on in my life. While I sat before my closed journal intent on praying for strength, I started to think about a meditation we held at the

Meeting House several years ago. I sometimes think my community can loosely be divided into those who meditate and and those who pray, and if that is the case them I am definitely of the praying ilk. It is second nature to me, I have done it for so long. I even remember once watching a football match on TV with Karl, England versus China I think, and Karl was very keen England should win. Ten minutes before the end we lost our lead, we were two all, and I caught myself praying that we would score! I was not being flippant. It is just that if you have spent a lifetime talking to someone about everything, you go on talking to him (or her) about everything, perhaps for the rest of your life. The amusing thing is that we did win the match.

Anyhow, I have tried meditation quite a lot, and I sometimes find it helpful, if rather self-centred compared with prayer, which is by definition centred on God by whatever name you call him. That particular evening we were doing a short, guided exercise in which we stood away in stages from our problems, or perhaps more accurately from a particular problem chosen in advance. We were supposed to get to the point where we could look at the issue we had selected from a distance, quite objectively, and no longer feel as if we owned the trouble. I can't remember what my problem was, one of the slight difficulties with such exercises is that they more or less depend on everyone present having something in their life which isn't straightforward. In my experience that isn't always the case. Anyhow, I do remember trying to follow the steps as we were guided, moving further and further from the issue in my mind. Finally we were supposed to find ourselves on a hill, looking down into the valley where our difficulty was spread out on a tablecloth in a meadow, almost invisible from so far away, and dwarfed by the rolling hills of the imaginary scene. But the thing I remember from the evening, with a sense of sharp reality each time I recall it, is the feeling I had that I was not standing on the hill alone. In my imagination I was aware of someone next to me. I turned to see who was with me, and it was Christ. Even now, thinking about that evening, I am surprised. I do not think of the Christ figure normally

– I think of God, I think of Jesus, and most of all I think of the Spirit. In an odd sort of way it lends credibility to the experience. If I had made it up, I wouldn't have made it up like that!

I wish I had been keeping a journal in those days because I would love to be able to turn to the next morning's entry to see what I had written at the time. I could find out what the problem had been, too, since I have long since forgotten that detail. I have never told anyone in Meeting about the experience although I have shared it once or twice with comparative strangers. Sometimes now I wonder if I have exaggerated it, but that is my 'rational' brain speaking. The conviction of Truth which came with the experience is as real as ever.

I had just drifted into remembering that occasion, intending rather to concentrate on praying for strength, and for a moment, when I realised how my mind had wandered, I felt angry with myself. Then I understood. In that guided meditation I had been shown something. I had been shown that if I stand back from my problems and do not let them hold on to me, then they cannot govern my life. But more significantly, I had been shown that whatever and wherever my problems are, I am not alone.

If this were a novel or a testimony being given by someone in the sort of church I used to belong to, and definitely if this were an American movie, no doubt the story would continue with the claim that after that I felt peace, confidence and so on. Since I am trying to be scrupulously honest in this journal, I will have to say that I felt a bit better, slightly less stressed, a little more able to focus on the day ahead, but I still had an ache inside, a sort of nagging consciousness of Simon in a cell in the death watch area, knowing that on a certain day, at a certain time, unless there is a miracle he will be lawfully murdered.

In the middle of yesterday morning Andy's partner Terry brought round the books they had promised. It is a lovely selection, waiting on the sideboard now, ready to be taken over to the tent school this afternoon. She stayed for coffee (herb tea in her case) and it was good to talk about the children at Meeting instead of the things that were really on my mind. I have decided that I will not tell anyone about Simon, unless the conversation turns so strongly in that direction that it is odd not to mention him. We talked about the pressure our kids are under at school, having to sift through what they hear at home and decide what to say in class or to their friends, and when to keep quiet. Terry thinks it is tougher for kids now than it used to be, but I am not sure. Childhood has always been a challenging time for minorities, and more children that you might think are in a minority one way or another.

In the afternoon we knitted a little and talked a lot. Sabina is going to be a great asset. She and Imran have discussed the whole project in a lot of detail and Sabina came with a list of 'provisions' they feel they can supply, including exercise books. Since there is no power connection over there, the kids in our school will have to write the old fashioned way instead of using DeVs, but we're not sure that is such a bad thing. There seems always to be a sort of moral panic around nowadays that children can no longer do maths without calculators, spell without spell checks or write without tablet prompts. Well, our kids will be able to do all those things! Imran collected Sabina and the baby just before five. He is a tall, slim man with a moustache and a small beard, and looks at his wife and child with a sort of deep joy.

So we have reached the great day. I will work at the shop this morning – I've switched with the manageress – and go to Meeting as usual but skip the lunch. Fran and I are teaching today, Jo and I tomorrow, Fran and Sabina on Friday and Jo and Sabina on Monday. We are planning to meet as always on Tuesday afternoons, primarily to plan, but to knit as well if we have the time. Once again I lift this venture to the Light, with thanksgiving.

Thursday 7th October

Karl rang last night. It was about 9.00pm, I had showered and washed my hair, and I was watching *Not Thinking of You* and laughing a lot. It is awful, but the events of the afternoon seem to have done a lot to help me get some perspective on Simon's date. Or is it awful that I have found this perspective? When governments commit murder, what sort of perspective should there be?

He asked a few cursory questions – how am I, have I seen Amy recently, that sort of thing. I haven't heard from Karl for weeks, not since the meatball meal. I asked him what he had been up to.

"Oh, I've been away," he said. "Work."

"Anywhere interesting?" I should have known better than to ask.

There was a slight pause then, "Milton Keynes," said Karl. He quite often gives me that answer. I have no idea whether it means 'mind your own business' or whether they have some sort of ATTF office or headquarters there.

"Right," I felt angry, mostly with myself for minding. He's only a friend, after all.

"So are you OK?" Karl persisted. I'd already told him I was fine. Then he added, "I heard about Simon."

I felt a little bit breathless. "How did you hear that?"

"It's all over the internet. Don't you ever look at the Amnesty site?" I do of course, but I wouldn't have expected Karl to. They list all the pending executions.

"Well, I'm a bit sad," I admitted. "And angry."

"Dinner on Friday then," Karl suggested. "I've got a trout in the freezer. Freshly caught. Fish is good for the brain. We can talk about it if you want."

I felt a surge of gratitude. I haven't spoken to anyone about Simon's date yet and here was Karl, the first one to make it impossible not to keep quiet any longer. I thought how unpredictable I find him, that he has checked on the Amnesty site. Did any of my other friends even think of it? Doesn't it show that despite the uncertainties of our friendship, Karl does really mind about me? There are times, even now, when I think that Karl is one of the best things ever to have happened to me. It seems silly now that I was in such a state about our relationship a few weeks ago. Karl is a good friend and he supplies something in my life which my community doesn't offer, a sort of balance. Friday will be comforting, and probably fun.

I wonder who gave Karl a fresh trout?

Both Fran and I thought the first lesson at the tent school went well yesterday. It was drizzling and quite cold. Our hopes of teaching the kids in the open air round the camp fire circle were obviously a non-starter, but Claire had cleared a space in their tent, which is a proper two-compartment camping tent designed for summer holidays, and we had four students for the first three quarters of an hour, and a fifth at the end. As planned we first sang songs together, and Claire and little Jamie showed us some new actions to go with a couple of them. Then we did some work with letters and sounds. One of Andy and Terry's books is a child's introduction to trees, so we collected leaves and identified the trees growing around their site. In a normal school we would put things up on the walls, but as we can't do that under these circumstances, we decided to keep a scrapbook log, so that the children can look through it and remind themselves what they have done.

I wondered if I would be out of my depth with such little ones, although of course I've had nieces and nephews and last Christmas I had quite a lot to do with some of Amy's grandchildren. Anyhow, I needn't have worried. There's a child called Pierre who seems very withdrawn, but perhaps he's just shy, and Sophie's speech isn't that good for a child of four, but they are lovely kids generally, and they all know Claire who stayed with us all the time. Jamie is a little star.

Afterwards Claire gave us some tea and the children drank water, then we headed back across the park feeling pleased. It seemed, at the same time, a very small thing to have done, and very important. That's probably me being melodramatic again.

Jo and I are teaching this afternoon. We agreed to meet up at the camp, because Jo can park by the old rugby club and walk across the back way. It is brighter today and maybe we can have our lessons outside, but it's already October, and quite cool.

Amy has emailed and asked me over for Sunday lunch. There aren't any Sunday buses any more, but she has a neighbour who worships at the cathedral, and he will give me a lift out after their service. Alec, he is called. I'll recognise him by the fact that he'll be smoking a pipe.

I turned over and looked at my clock at 3.30 this morning and suddenly I was wide awake. I do this sometimes and I know that there's no point in trying to sleep again for a while. At one time I used to go downstairs and play word games online, but in those days wakefulness was always accompanied by a sort of subdued panic. When I was teaching, life was one big battle against tiredness, and I knew that if I was awake in the night I'd be tired in the day, and if I were to be challenged by a difficult parent or a tricky classroom situation, I'd have nothing to fall back on. Once, more recently, after I'd moved to this flat, I watched a complete movie on line, something about child abuse, unwanted pregnancies and an inspirational teacher, all taking place in a grim part of New York City. If I can't sleep nowadays it is not a problem, I can just sleep later in the morning or nap after lunch. Last night when I woke up I didn't want to do anything electronic. I put my dressing gown on and wondered into the sitting room, pulling back the curtains and looking out.

It was a very dark night. When the leaves have fallen, light from the park will shine into the garden, but not yet, so there were grey-silver moon shadows and strange patches of pitch black. I pulled my chair up and sat looking out, my mind calm but feeling very alert.

There was a cat on the lawn. I suppose it was hunting, I watched it stalk something into the shadows of a shrub, then it did a remarkable jump, straight up in the air. There was more stalking, then another jump. I wondered if the little creature who was the prey knew that the cat was after it. Did it know how to escape? Finally the cat caught whatever it was and swung it round and round, shaking it. I suppose the little thing was dead by then. The cat dropped it, stood back, then pounced on it again. I had never thought before that hunting might be fun for creatures who catch their own food, just as fishing is somehow fun for the huntin' and fishin' brigade. It would be quite different if it were a matter of survival. I don't suppose the cat would have played with the mouse if it hadn't eaten all day.

After the cat had gone I sat for a long time, staring into the dark. In the last few years I have learnt to let thoughts and ideas pass through my mind, the way I might at the beginning of Meeting, glancing at each thought but not dwelling on anything unless one picture or idea pushes itself into the foreground. I thought about the tent school and especially one little girl dressed in pink dungarees, who had talked repeatedly about 'my house'.

"In my house we have a television and a Smart DeV47x," she said. Later it was, "In my house my mummy makes biscuits. We eat them for tea." It was difficult to know how to answer her. Afterwards Claire told Jo that Felicity lived in the corrugated iron lean-to at the edge of the camp, the construction with the blue tarpaulin over it.

Another picture that came into my mind was from Wednesday, in the shop. This city has some seriously wealthy people in it, and it surprises me how often they look round the shop. A woman came in with a teenager wearing the St. Jude the Less uniform. I was behind the counter sorting through jewellery and attaching tiny price labels. The woman and teenager talked to each other as if I were not there.

"Hey look, Granny – do you like this waistcoat?" It was on the men's rail, but teenagers are wearing big, colourful waistcoats this autumn. We've sold several.

Granny had a look at the garment in question. "It's silk," she pronounced, "but a bit scruffy. When would you wear it?"

"At Ginny's party. It's only three dollars."

Granny was not convinced. "That shop at the top of town has new ones," she remarked. "Green would suit you better than that yellow, it's a bit sickly. Let me treat you – you deserve it after that awful dentist. Then some lunch, I think, before I take you back to school."

I was remembering Claire, who is not so much older than this kid, and thinking how people literally don't know how the other half live. I was feeling critical of their region-less accents and confident poises.

As they left the girl turned and smiled to me. "Thank you anyhow," she said.

Next I started thinking about cowboys. This is not as odd as it sounds, because I had watched a programme about American country music. I had been struck by the fact that governors of huge states nowadays, people with the power of life and death over others, dress the way poor singers dressed in the 1950s and 60s. That the poor might emulate the rich I could, in theory, understand, but I don't think that's what happens. I think the rich eventually copy the poor. That, when you think about it, is strange.

My thoughts changed direction again when my DeV made that familiar little 'beep' they make when they log in, and then it made another noise, slightly deeper and more drawn out, not so much a beep as an electronic sigh. I have not consciously noticed it doing that before, but it sounded familiar. Perhaps it has always made that noise too? Or maybe it has been upgraded, that happens all the time. I really don't understand electronic devices at all. After that I went back to bed and slept deeply until after seven this morning.

Today will be a busy day, but not as bad as Wednesday. I need to open the shop at 10.00am, and I usually buy my groceries on Fridays. Karl will pick me up around 4.30pm, so I'll have time to shower. I'll buy some wine on the way home. Karl's bound to have bought some, but it doesn't hurt to have extra bottles in the house. I'd normally really look forward to a day like today. Everything except the grocery shopping is enjoyable one way or another, but I'm aware of having a slight sick feeling, and I think it's to do with Simon. Each day brings him that much closer to his death, and the knowledge of it drags on my heart, like a load I'm pulling behind me. I half wish I were teaching at the tent school today, too, but Fran and Sabina will be fine. I need to recognise and reject this desire always to be in control.

Karl was really lovely yesterday evening, it was almost as if we were a proper item again. Almost. He was wearing jeans and a jumper I haven't seen before, his hair short and spiky, quite military. There must have been lovely weather in Milton Keynes because he has a tan. His flat looks good too. Karl is funny about his flat. Sometimes it seems quite messy, with books and papers everywhere and no sign of anyone having cleaned up for weeks, but sometimes, like last night, it is obvious that he's been round with the hoover and bleach. It was tidy, clean and inviting.

He never lets me do anything in the kitchen, which I really like. I don't just mean that Karl doesn't want me to cook, he doesn't like me washing up either. It was barely five when we got there, so we had a cup of tea and watched some cricket until Karl handed me the remote and went off to prepare the meal.

We each had a gin and tonic first, and the fish was cooked whole in a light pastry case, with asparagus and new potatoes. We didn't drink my wine. Karl said a polite 'thank you' and took it into the kitchen. Later he served something Portuguese. He said it went well with fish. He was right.

Afterwards I expected we'd watch a film or channel hop, or possibly (which I don't like) turn back to the cricket. Instead Karl poured the last of the wine into our glasses and said, "Let's talk, shall we?"

In real life I don't think people say 'let's talk' very often. They say, "Were you going to tell me about ..." or "Have you thought about..." or "I wanted to ask you..." and then you know what to say. 'Let's talk', sounds like the beginning of a counselling session, and I had no idea how to start.

We were sitting on the long settee, Karl turned sideways to look at me. "You knew it was bound to happen, didn't you? I mean with Simon?"

"Yes." Of course I did. Why did I feel he was telling me off?

He didn't say anything, just looked straight at me. His

expression was kind, but a bit distant. I looked over his shoulder, out of the window. "I knew it was going to happen sooner or later," I agreed, "but I hoped it would be later. Actually, I hoped it wouldn't happen at all." I found myself sighing. "So now I'll just have to get on with it."

Karl sighed too. "I hate the idea of you having to get on with it," he said. Then, a bit forcefully, "It's ridiculous! Why do you get into these situations?" Then, more calmly, "There's so much someone like you could do without all this grief," he said. "Look at Amy!"

"I know, I know." I agreed. It's something I don't understand myself. The tent school, Simon, both are a little extreme. I thought of my community, of people in the old days refusing to wear dyed cloth because the dye workers were badly treated, or campaigning against slavery, or against missiles at Greenham Common. Did I join the community because I was already like-minded, or do I gravitate to the edges of society because of their influence?

Karl was still looking at me, the same kind, serious expression on his face. "I wish you wouldn't," he said. "I really don't think you should do all these ... get involved in the stuff you do. After this, after Simon, will you give yourself a break? Would you think about it? I thought you might take up painting when you retired. Do you remember, we talked about it." He swivelled round so that he was looking straight ahead at the blank television screen. "You could have such a good retirement, if only ..."

I didn't know what to say. Sitting in Karl's flat it seemed true. I had wanted to start painting, maybe water-colours, and I am very content just pottering around my flat, reading, knitting, doing my stints in the shop, going to Meeting – Karl didn't even know about the tent school, but of course he wouldn't approve. It sounded very attractive, a quiet, settled retirement in a pleasant flat in a cathedral city, with a sister-in-law close by and a kind (if elusive) man to cook me meals and take an interest ... "Well, that might be a good idea," I agreed. "I don't think I want to go through this again in a hurry." When I said it, thinking about Simon, I meant it.

Karl turned back to me and smiled. He almost grinned, he really did look very pleased. "We could think about going away somewhere," he said. "A short trip, if you'd like it, when … after Simon … maybe in February? Depending on my work."

"OK," I agreed and finished my wine.

Will we really go away somewhere? When I first knew Karl we talked about it a bit, but of course then I was teaching and somehow my holidays and his never seemed to coincide. Last night it seemed like a lovely idea, but more of a dream than a genuine plan. Today I feel pleased that Karl suggested it, but I find I have a reservation in my mind. Should I really be getting closer to him?

Well, all I can do is live with the idea of a trip and see how it develops, if at all. In the meantime today I want to do some lesson preparation and also read an epistle that has come from North America. Our communities there have huge problems and it is easy to forget that other societies, having moved further to the right than we have, are presenting good, peaceable people with dilemmas we have not had to face here for centuries. A Meeting House in Arizona has been burned to the ground. Fire experts have concluded that it was accidental and the insurance company has declared that the Meeting was in default on the premiums for their premises. The fire occurred less than a week after the community organised a demonstration concerning the poor diets of prisoners in that state. It is the third Meeting House fire in the south west in as many months. At the Business Meeting the epistle was circulated along with a report from our central organisation and we were asked all to read it and to consider whether we should donate something to the rebuilding that will be necessary. I think I have to take this pretty seriously because Arizona is in some ways not dissimilar to Texas where Simon is imprisoned, and things were getting pretty rough there two years ago, when I last visited.

I think I will walk into town too, to buy some chocolates to take to lunch tomorrow. It is one of those crisp, cold mornings which remind me that a frost might come soon, in a month or so.

I feel less jittery today. I wonder if I am becoming used to the idea of Simon's execution or whether I am benefiting from Karl's obvious concern? I would hate to think that I might be the sort of person who, in the balance of a human life on one hand and the friendly concern of an attractive man on the other, would be more affected by the attractive man. Before I do anything else I think I will spend some time in stillness, opening myself to the Spirit, to bring about those changes in me which I cannot create in myself.

Monday 11th October

I didn't write this journal yesterday (obviously). I hardly ever do on a Sunday. When I first started going to Meeting we met in a hall across the road from the Meeting House at 10.00am each Sunday. The hall was often quite full, but following the crack-down after the Brazilian Olympics and the New Alliance, we had an influx of new worshippers, mostly from other churches. It was impossible then to house us all in one Worship Meeting, so we split into two, and later three. We consider ourselves to be one community and there is quite a lot of movement between meetings, although generally younger people and single people seem to favour the evening meeting. I like the 9.00am slot. I love the short walk across town and past the children's playground, and I enjoy the cathedral bells and the smell of coffee from the café by the Guildhall. There are some lovely and some venerable people who attend that early meeting, and I like the gentleness with which the young homeless are greeted when, as is increasingly the case, they come to sit in the porch and drink the coffee our warden makes. The murmur of their conversation just outside the meeting room seems no more disruptive than the cooing of the pigeons or, sometimes, the barking of a dog. There is often ministry. Yesterday one of our newer members stood, about twenty minutes into the meeting, and spoke about something she had recently read, a quotation from Luke's Gospel, 'The Spirit of the Lord is on me'. She spoke about what it meant to her to experience the Spirit on her, and how she and her husband, who is not part of our community, felt that they should take her husband's parents into their home, now that the benefits of the older couple had been withdrawn. She spoke of the peace they felt from making the right decision. Later someone else spoke about the difference between doing something because you knew in your head it is right, or doing it because you know in your heart it's right. The latter, she said, is the Spirit. I would have liked to have shared about our little school, because I know we are agreed that the Spirit has led us in this, but I also know we have to be careful about what we say in open meetings. Nevertheless, I felt a deep sense of peace and completeness.

I met Alec, Amy's friend, outside the main entrance to the cathedral. He is absolutely typical of the people Amy seems to gather round her. Matins at the cathedral does not start until 10.30am, so even after I had crossed the road to the Meeting House for coffee, passed the epistle and report on to Rob, discussed it with Maisy and Hans, and helped the warden stack the coffee cups from the homeless and the people in First Meeting into the dish washer, I was still early. As soon as Alec came out of the big door to the right talking to a woman in robes and a dog collar, he lit his pipe and glanced around, as if looking for me. I went over and asked, "Are you Alec?"

He took his pipe out of his mouth, patted the hand of the priest to whom he had been speaking, and said to me, "Ah-ha! You must be Amy's black sheep!" He settled a tweed cap on his head, so that he looked for all the world like a farmer from a very old series of *In the English Countryside*, nodded in the general direction of the cathedral close and said, "The car's over there, parked by the school."

I suppose Alec is about seventy, definitely ex-public school and ex-army, and really very good company. All the way out to the village he regaled me with ridiculous stories about mistakes made by clergy when reciting the liturgy or giving sermons, or by ordinary members of the congregation when reading from the Bible. The lovely thing about Alec's conversation, apart from the fact that he spoke so beautifully, was that although it was all really funny he was definitely not poking fun at anyone. I got the feeling he just found life incurably amusing. He drove with one hand on the wheel and sucked at his pipe between sentences, glancing sideways at me with twinkling eyes now and again. Some of his stories were obviously quite old and well rehearsed. He still spoke about pounds and pence instead of dollars and cents, and he called policemen 'Bobbies'. I can really understand why Amy likes him.

Lunch was fun. Amy's house was full of people: Alec's quiet, plump wife was there, along with Amy's daughter Meggan, looking a bit harassed, her son-in-law Hugh, and their three children. There was also an elderly lady in a green flowery dress who was introduced to me simply as Louise, and who said almost nothing the whole time I was there. We started with drinks before lunch, and ate a full four-course meal which started with fingers of toast covered in pâté and cucumber and ended with biscuits, cheese and grapes, with roast pork as the main course. It was half past three by the time we sat down to coffee (which the children made) and I felt I might never need to eat again. The talk was mostly about the village, although Alec and his wife had that sort of good manners which meant that they asked me intelligent questions about education and about my flat, which is eco-friendly and modern. Somehow the conversation was steered to politically safe topics in an apparently effortless way, and Alec's stream of funny stories continued gently throughout. I could see that Meggan's children loved Alec, and the youngest one spent quite a lot of time close to Louise too. After sherry before lunch and a glass of wine it all looked very attractive, and I could see why people choose to live in these pretty Hampshire villages. It was only in Hugh's car coming home, when we passed all those 'to let' signs, that I thought again of the tents in the park, and realised that, however warm and friendly Amy's circle of family and friends might seem, I could not really live like that.

It is another pleasant day today. Some of the leaves of the trees around the garden are turning orange and brown, although others are still green with that dark hue of late summer. It must be cooler because the smart heating is quite warm at my feet and the up-draft of the heat is making the curtains to the French windows move a little. I slept well last night. I drank quite a lot yesterday and ate a huge amount, and when I got in, in the evening, I watched a really interesting programme about the history of a Welsh choir, which included some beautiful music. I still feel a little lurch inside me when I think of Simon, but that feeling of dread no longer sits in my stomach. Sabina and Jo are doing the school this morning so I will have a 'normal' Monday. I'll clean the flat when I've done this, and spend the afternoon at the shop. I think I might cut some sprays of leaves and make an arrangement for the dining table in the corner.

I lift all these matters to the Light.

Tuesday 12th October

I had a letter from Simon again this morning. The post came surprisingly early. He rarely writes this often, but perhaps now I will hear from him more. This letter must have overlapped with my card. He asks me to go out and visit one more time. He asks me, rather tentatively, whether I will be there to witness his execution.

I am stunned. I think I am frightened. This does not seem real. I do not want to do it.

Visiting Texas has become a really difficult project. At conferences I have spoken to people who used to go often, but of course the situation over there has deteriorated in the last few years. Last time I went it was really uncomfortable. My credit and debit cards wouldn't work anywhere outside Houston, for one thing. The ATMs are different from ours, and ask you to put in your zip code. If you don't have a zip code they won't give you money. I spent ages tracking round to banks in the town where the prison is located, trying just to get some cash. It is no longer wise for a foreigner to drive over there either, although to be honest I was never comfortable hiring a car in the States, because I don't often drive here. In the last few years there have been several high profile cases when foreigners (including that British diplomat, Gregory someone) have been involved in relatively minor road traffic incidents and have ended up in jail, and then it is a real struggle to get them free. It was three weeks before that Gregory guy's wife even discovered where he was. On my last visit I used taxis all the while, but that is expensive and my accent gives me away as a foreigner, so that I was cross-examined a couple of times by fairly aggressive drivers who seemed to hold me personally responsible for the situation in the Caribbean.

Simon's request fills me with dread. I dread the immigration procedure, I dread the xenophobia, I dread Karl's reaction to Simon's request, I dread the time between now and January 12th, but of course what I really dread is seeing Simon murdered. I feel sick with dread.

Nevertheless, even as I write this I realise that I will have to go. I want to go.

The jittery feeling is back with a vengeance. This afternoon we four are meeting to discuss the school, and I will have to tell the others about Simon, and as soon as I have written this journal I will reply to Simon and then email Karl. Then I should check with the airlines. Is it wise to book a flight yet? It is still three months before Simon is due to die, and the system is famous for granting (reluctantly) last minute reprieves. But I can't afford to leave it too late and then not get a flight, now that the availability of seats for civilians is so reduced. I will need to get clearance to enter the country too, and that is no longer a forgone conclusion. The whole project seems daunting.

For a minute I find myself angry with Simon. How could he ask this of me? But at once I feel shame. Didn't I tell him that I believed in him? That I would do anything I could to help him? Don't I already know that his daughter has dropped out of his life and he will be alone? So, I don't want to do this. What has that to do with anything? Life is full of things we don't want to do. It is time I started thinking of someone other than myself.

If ever there was a time for settling myself in peace, this is it. I will sit here at the window and I will not move until I have let go of all these negative feelings. If the disciplines of my community mean anything, then I can do this.

Wednesday 13th October

I did not sleep well last night. Yesterday morning I checked flights to Texas and emailed the prison, asking the correct protocol if I wanted to attend Simon's execution. I emailed Karl, and after a bit of thought, I emailed the clerk of Meeting and Amy too. Then I sat and looked at the DeV47 screen (which in this little flat is also the projector for my TV screen). I struggled and struggled to find peace, but found, in the end, a sort of numbness. I want to be honest in this journal, but I really do not understand my own feelings at all. I know I can be very melodramatic about things, and I fear that is what I'm doing now: indulging myself. But how do I stop?

I couldn't eat lunch. When Jo, Fran and Sabina arrived I found it really hard to do all the social niceties, like taking their jackets and cooing over little Yasmin and sorting out drinks. As soon as we were sitting down (all with paper notebooks at the ready, no DeVs in sight) I told them about Simon.

Jo and Fran, of course, know quite a lot about him. Over the last four and a half years I have spoken about him often, and it was Fran who picked me up from the airport two years ago when I last visited. Nevertheless, they were all surprised, because I had stuck to my resolution not to mention his execution date unless the conversation turned strongly in that direction, and of course we tend to talk mostly about the school and the tent dwellers nowadays. All three of them looked pretty serious, but it was Sabina who said what had been vaguely forming in my mind all morning,

"I don't think they'll let you in to visit. Texas … Imran won't apply to go there any more, they're very suspicious, you know."

"I went two years ago," I pointed out. "They asked a lot of questions at immigration and typed a lot of stuff into their computer, but they let me in."

"That was two years ago, though," said Fran. "All this business in the Caribbean hadn't blown up then."

"Have you ever belonged to Amnesty?" Jo asked.

"No. I always think I should join but I just never did," I confessed.

"Good. And do you belong to a political party?"

"No, but you know I was a union rep … but that was when I was working. They knew that last time I went there."

"I hope they don't let you in," said Sabina, suddenly sounding very fierce. "Better that, than that they don't let you out!"

"Do you think you can do it?" asked Jo. "Watch someone be killed, I mean?"

We all went quiet. That, of course, is the crunch question.

"I think I have to," I said. "It's a bit late to start counting the cost."

Sabina said, "Imran and I will pray for you," then, seeing the alarm on my face she added, "privately, on our own. We won't talk about this."

After that we planned the work for the next week, and Jo showed us the scrapbook which logs the children's work. We have seven students now: Jamie, Sophie, Pierre and Felicity have been there from the start, and Nellie came in at the very end of our first session, then missed two afternoons, but was there again this Monday with her mother, who talked to Sabina before they started. She was worried in case we were keeping records, but Sabina showed her the children's scrapbook, which doesn't include any last names, and Nellie's mother seemed reassured. Trent and Julius are older than the others. Trent is seven and started on Friday, his brother Julius is nine, and both can read and write, although it is obvious, Jo says, that they learnt on DeVs. It shows in the way they hold their pencils. We spent some time talking about how to integrate the older boys, and about the need to teach them how to use pens and pencils efficiently. I must say, for the first time I feel a little sympathy for the 'back to basics' conservative lobby, who want to ban tablets from primary schools.

Another good development is Alfred. I thought he was really quite old. Well, perhaps he is, but I forget that I am a retired woman myself now! Alfred has volunteered to play his banjo when we sing with the children. He demonstrated to Sabina and Fran after they had finished yesterday, and they say he plays and sings, and knows some of the songs we have been teaching the children. It seems he listened to our lessons. We all feel this is a very positive development, because the school is becoming a joint venture. Claire is always there, and Nellie's mother shows signs of wanting to be involved, and now Alfred. And Jo told us that Johnny has spoken to her about the possibility he raised in our Business Meeting, of maybe teaching some science in the evenings. He asked that we get back to him by word of mouth, he doesn't want anything in writing. Johnny, of course, is in employment and must be really careful. We discussed his brave proposal and think it might be good if he just teaches Trent and Julius to begin with, maybe on Tuesday evenings, since there are no other lessons on Tuesdays.

When the others left Jo gave me a big hug, which is a little unusual. I made a meal (I eat vegetarian food on Tuesdays and Thursdays) and watched some fairly mindless television, trying to calm down. I checked my emails. The clerk has said we might tell the next Business Meeting about my proposed trip to Texas, and he asks how the school is going, which means that despite all our efforts there is an electronic record now. I had an email from Karl too, which simply asks, in response to my morning announcement that I was planning to go to Simon's execution, "Is this wise?" I am a little disappointed with his response, after he was so caring at the weekend, but of course I knew he wouldn't approve. There was no reply from Amy.

Although I don't sleep well I usually fall asleep as soon as I turn out my light. I often wake several times, sometimes for long periods in the early hours of the morning. Last night, though, I just could not settle. Sometimes, if the air is particularly still, I can hear noises from quite far away: trains on the fast London to Southampton line, or music from someone else's flat or even from the Tavern. I lay there listening to these noises, and to the lift going up to the second floor and back, and to the little bleeps and sighs of my DeV phone which I had left charging in the kitchen. I could not relax. I found myself running through tomorrow's lesson plan, and thinking about what I will need to do if I go to Texas. I turned on the radio, but I feel the news is so biased nowadays that I no longer trust what I hear, and so I turned it off again. I heard the clock of St Bartholomew's strike midnight and I was beginning to think I would get up again, when at last I started to feel sleepy. I dreamt a long, muddled dream about checking in for a flight and not having the right paperwork, until I woke up at seven this morning, feeling a bit sick and rather disgruntled.

Well, I will go to Meeting at lunch time and then straight across to the park for school at 1.30pm. I will need to take the scrapbook, which we left here yesterday, and the books about rivers.

Thursday 14th *October*

Two good things have happened since I wrote this journal yesterday. First, Johnny came round in the evening and we talked about him teaching the boys science. He will start next Tuesday. And this morning I had an email from the prison giving me permission to witness Simon's execution. Well, really three good things have happened, since school yesterday afternoon was great. We started with singing, which is our custom, and Alfred taught us all a new song. I think it is a really old protest song, with the refrain, "We're low, we're low, we're very, very low," and the kids loved it. Jamie knows all the letters of the alphabet now, and recognises his name, and the children spent quite a lot of their time during our three o'clock break looking at last week's work in the scrapbook, which Sabina and Jo had put together after Monday's lessons. We looked at trees last week and we're going to spend a week on rivers, then on river birds. We hope that by focussing on their environment we will legitimise it for the children, so that their camp feels less temporary, or less accidental. At the end of the afternoon we taught them 'Row, row, row your boat', with actions. It looks as if Trent wants to learn how to play the banjo.

I slept a little better last night. I was very tired. I went to sleep quickly but I was awake at five and I only dozed until 6.30am, when I gave up and made breakfast. Jo and I are teaching this afternoon and I want to do an hour in the shop this morning, since I am no longer working there on Wednesday afternoons. Fortunately we seem to have a lot of volunteers just now so I don't feel I've left them in the lurch. I still feel a bit queasy but nothing like as bad as I felt yesterday morning. A friend I met two years ago in the visitors' room at the prison, who has herself attended an execution, has seen Simon's date on the Amnesty website and emailed me this morning asking if I am planning to go out there, as if it were the most natural thing in the world, and that has done more than anything to calm me down, and I had a text from Amy which must have arrived while I was asleep, 'Be strong! Love and hugs!' Three months from now it will all be over. I can do this.

Friday 15th October

Something strange happened yesterday. I don't know whether to worry about it, or not. I had a pile of ironing to do in the morning, and did it right after writing yesterday's journal entry, then I thought I would pop into the Meeting House to see whether the new greeting rota was in my pigeon hole (I forgot to check on Wednesday) and to buy some more yoghurt on my way back. I bumped into Sky by the market, and as we stood there talking a guy came up to us. I cannot remember that I have ever seen him or spoken to him before. He was wearing a big green waxed jacket and a woolly hat pulled down to cover his hair completely, and his eyes were vaguely Asiatic in appearance.

"Hello, sisters," he said, "planning the revolution?"

Sky looked at me as if to say, "Who is this?" and I said, "I beg your pardon?"

The guy in the green jacket said, "Oh, I know you two! Out to change the world! Up the workers!" Then he left, walking off behind the flower stall.

Sky said, "Who was *that*?"

I had no idea. Was it one of the rough sleepers who drinks coffee in the porch during First Meeting? Does he live at the tent encampment? I am bad at remembering faces, he might have been there, dressed differently, some time when I've been in the park.

It made us both feel very uneasy. "Perhaps he's seen me at the Feeding Station," suggested Sky.

"Or he might have seen me at Meeting," I commented. "A big online paper did an article about our National Meeting in August, We were called 'revolutionaries' there …"

"But he talked as if he knew us…" Sky had a frown of worry.

"We don't do anything illegal," I pointed out. "This is still a free country!" Nevertheless I was feeling pretty uncomfortable.

I thought about the guy as I walked home. In a way it would be quite encouraging to be thought a revolutionary, if by that he only meant that I wanted to change the world, or my corner of it, for the better. But that isn't what 'revolutionary' means any more, if it ever did. It seems to me that as we have moved further away from values of the mid-twentieth century, the word 'revolution' has taken on a host of unattractive associations. In school kids are taught about the revolutions at the beginning of the twentieth century as wholly bad experiences, as if there were no idealism or desire for fairer societies involved, and as if they achieved nothing good at all. Then, at the beginning of the twenty-first century, somehow anti-capitalist grass roots movements became associated in the public mind with both 'revolution' and terrorism. When the ATTF was first set up and there was a lot of media chatter about this new Anti Terrorism Task Force, it was unclear whether the terrorists from whom we were to be protected were religious fanatics or anti-capitalists, or even hunt saboteurs! Now the word 'revolution' has connotations of threat, when I suppose originally it meant change for the better. A similar thing has happened with the word 'reform'. It used to refer to improvements. The early reforms in the nineteenth century stopped children from working long hours, stopped electoral corruption, stopped men and women from being paid at different rates simply because of their gender, and so on. 'Reform' was about making life better for the ordinary citizen. In the early years of this century 'reform' came to have the opposite meaning. The health reforms led to the situation we have now where doctors are reluctant to diagnose or treat intractable or long term illnesses because of their budgets, and benefit reform meant poor people were given less help. The education reforms made a good education harder for ordinary people to access, and the recent rent reforms have made thousands of families homeless. 'Reform' now carries implications of danger, of uncertainty, of ordinary people losing control of their lives.

So if a stranger comes up to me and tells me I am a revolutionary, I feel as I might if I had been told I am a scrounger or a bad neighbour. It is like saying that I want to disrupt the orderly life of our country.

The other worrying thing is that neither of us knew who that guy was. I am an ordinary retired woman with unremarkable dress sense living quietly in a cathedral city. Sky is a hard working person with a big social conscience. Neither of us are the sort of people who are recognised in the street. As I walked back to the flat I felt as if I were notorious, and it was a very uncomfortable feeling.

The feeling stayed with me through school in the afternoon. I was working with Jo, and since it was not raining we were able to do the outdoor version of our lesson, looking at the direction of the river flow by throwing Pooh sticks in from the wooden bridge. We looked at how the letter 'W' looks like waves on water, and we made a collage for the log book. We had a little victory this afternoon too. Little Felicity, the child who keeps talking about 'my house' as if she still lives in a proper brick-built home with a kitchen and a bathroom, has caused us some concern. When we talked on Tuesday afternoon we discovered that we had all had these conversations with Felicity about the good things she does in her house, and we felt we just did not know whether this is normal and we should accept it, or whether we were in some way colluding with an unhealthy inability to adapt by going along with what she said.

This afternoon, though, when we had our break (milk and

biscuits today, thanks to Jo) the children started talking about who lived closest to the river. There was a disagreement between Jamie and Sophie, which Claire solved by getting the children to count the number of steps from their respective tents to the nearest point on the bank (Jamie is closest). Then Felicity said, "I am not closest. My house is furthest away!" And then, to prove her point, she paced the number of steps from the hut with the blue tarpaulin to the river bank. I think, actually, Trent and Julius live further from the bank than Felicity does, but that is hardly the point. Felicity was claiming the hut as her home.

All the same, the morning's conversation with green-jacket man left a shadow on my day. As school drew to an end various tent dwellers started returning to the camp, and I found myself looking at each person as he or she arrived, half hoping it would be him. Then at least I would know how he knew me. About half the adults were back by the time I left, including a couple I hadn't seen before with a baby in a sling, but not that man. I described him to Claire, or rather I described his clothes and his eyes, but she had no idea who he might have been.

Although Sky keeps a low profile in the city, a lot of poorer people know what she does because of the Feeding Station, but are there people outside my circle of friends who know that I go over to the tent settlement? Do they know we've started a school? It bothered me all yesterday evening.

Saturday 16th October

The Eastern European couple who do the garden came early today. It is not quite nine in the morning and they are already working away down there, clearing beds and tidying the whole area ready for winter. I am sitting at my closed French window and they saw me and waved up in their usual friendly fashion. They are very industrious.

Yesterday was a much less bothersome day than Thursday. When I walked into the shop for my usual Friday morning slot I found myself looking all around me, wandering if I would see the man with the green jacket again. There were quite a lot of people around including a crowd of teenagers. The market was busy. In the last few years there have been more and more tray people. I think they are not really traditional market stall holders at all. They walk slowly around wearing large trays which are strapped to their shoulders like portable counters, and they spread out their wares and hope people will buy. I suspect that, unlike the real stall holders, the tray people don't pay for their pitches. Sometimes their selections of goods are quite interesting. Last Christmas I bought little hand-sewn cloth containers for putting handbag-sized packets of tissues in, from one of these tray people. At other times the stuff on their trays is pathetic. I saw a girl once who seemed to be trying to sell all the contents of her make-up drawer, and this morning someone was trying to sell items that looked like second-hand Christmas decorations – in October! I suppose people do what they have to do when food is short.

I kept an eye on the door of the shop too, for the first hour, still worried in case the man came in, but of course he didn't. Then, around morning coffee time we had a huge drop-off of goods for resale, real quality clothes, some scarves and two pairs of beautiful, sparkling evening sandals. The student (Rolf) who was working with me was really funny. He went into ecstasies over the dresses and I thought he was going to pass out with joy when he saw the sandals! We priced them quite high ($15 for one of the dresses) but even so we sold several items by lunch time. The profits from the shop traditionally go to developing countries, but a questionnaire in the form of a colourful hand-out has appeared in the last couple of days asking anyone who donates or buys goods from us to express their opinion about whether we should start to retain a proportion for the very poor in England. Rolf and I both voted 'yes' before we handed over to Dolly, the manageress, at lunch time. It wasn't until I got home that I realised I had stopped worrying about the man, and now all sorts of common-sense explanations have popped into my head. Maybe green-jacket man just assumed I was a 'revolutionary' because I was talking to Sky. Maybe he had just heard the word on some alternative music track. I am altogether too paranoid!

Today I am going to book my flight to Texas, and the hotels in Houston and in Stanley where the prison is located. After lunch I want to knit the last three squares for our current blanket, sew them up and crochet a border, so that Fran can drop off the completed article at the convent next week. It has taken us much longer to knit this blanket than the last, even though Sabina has joined the group. It is because of the school, of course. Then I plan to do some serious reading for the book group. I don't expect to go out at all today.

Monday 18th October

Our warden and a couple of our young people had made bacon sandwiches to go with the coffee for the homeless yesterday, and when I arrived at Meeting it smelt lovely! Our hall is long and low, close to one branch of the river and to a weir, and I felt calm and peaceful sitting there, opening my heart and listening to the sound of the water, to the pigeons, and to the homeless people in the porch talking quietly and once hooting with laughter and then stopping very suddenly. I suppose someone had reminded them what we were doing on the other side of the door. Two of the street people and one of their dogs came into the meeting and sat in the back row. I wonder what they make of us?

After Meeting, though, I had a real shock. We end our meetings when two elders shake hands, and then we have some sharing of thoughts and news, and notices, before straightening out the chairs for the next meeting and heading back across the road for coffee. No sooner had the assistant clerk said, "You are all welcome to go across to the Meeting House for coffee," than the person in front of me (Josh, I think) turned and said, "I see your tent people are in the news again."

"What?" I said, "What's happened?"

"Didn't you see the *Messenger* on Friday?" Josh said (or is he

Jeremy?). "There was a big article about the tent settlement and about local concerns. It said the neighbourhood are up in arms. It isn't safe to let children play in the park. You know the sort of thing. There'll be a copy of the paper in the Meeting House, I'm sure."

I could hardly wait to get across there and see for myself. I won't exaggerate in this journal, so I won't say it was worse than I had feared, but it was certainly pretty bad. There was a big coloured photograph of the camp with two snarling dogs in the foreground, and a long article about the encampment. The language was typical newspaper language. The tent dwellers were not 'homeless' they were 'riff-raff'. Their dwellings were not tents and makeshift huts, they were 'squalid eye-sores' and the adults were not parents trying desperately to keep their families together against all the odds, and still holding down steady jobs in many cases, they were scroungers, layabouts and benefit fraudsters. Several members of the public had consented to be interviewed, and had expressed concern, disgust, indignation and rage that such people should be allowed to camp in the park. A city official had maintained that the authorities are 'aware' of the situation and are 'monitoring it carefully'. The elected chief constable (no doubt aware of his popularity ratings) promised that the police would act at the slightest hint of trouble or criminality The vicar of St. Bartholomew's church reminded everyone that we have a huge problem with homelessness in the city and that in a couple of months we will be celebrating Christmas, and of the story of Jesus being born in a stable because his parents had no home, and the interviewer himself or herself had added 'but it is unclear whether Rev Florence McNutt's congregation would feel the same generosity of spirit.'

The part that bothered me as much as anything else, however, came where the journalist had interviewed some of the tent dwellers themselves. Someone called Walter was reported as saying that if there is trouble at the camp or in the park it will be the responsibility of the city council and of central government, since they have created the problem of homelessness in the first place. This is bound to upset all sorts of powerful people. Even worse, someone else had said, 'We are not scroungers or lazy people. We are doing our best in difficult circumstances. We have formed a collective. We are pooling our resources. We have established a school for our children and some local people are helping us, we are keeping our site clean…' So now the school is really out in the open.

I wanted to talk to Fran and Jo but they both go to Second Meeting so that their children can be at the children's class. I didn't want to discuss the newspaper article over coffee because I had no idea who some of the people were, standing or sitting, drinking the warden's good coffee and discussing (of all things) this year's apple harvest. Then I thought I would go across the park on my way home and see if Claire or Alfred were there…

As soon as I got past the bowling club hut I knew I could make no such visit yesterday morning. There were three police officers in yellow jackets standing about half way down the football pitch, one apparently speaking on a little DeV phone. There was a small crowd of people, mostly white-haired, standing in a cluster near the path to the flats. A group of teenage boys with their fashionable multi-coloured canes and long jackets was standing close to the river, and I could see several people on the little wooden bridge. Nothing seemed actually to be happening. I thought I had either just missed something, or arrived just in time to see whatever was about to occur.

I stood there for a moment taking stock, when a voice said, "Hello, you're up and about early!"

I turned to see Judy from the flats, with two of her grandchildren. She looked rosy cheeked and cheerful. The little girl was clutching a paper bag. "We came down to feed the ducks," explained Judy, "but we seem to have walked right into an incident!"

"What's happening?" I asked, my mouth feeling dry.

"Oh, I don't know. Sean, don't eat the bread, it's for the ducks!" Then she said, "They'll be giving those poor folks trouble, as if they hadn't fallen on hard enough times already."

We stood and watched for a minute or two. The little girl said, "Granny, why are those policemen there?"

Nothing seemed to be happening. Then two of the men from the group of white-haired people walked purposefully across to the police officers and seemed to have some sort of conversation. They returned to their group, looking angry. A woman officer walked across to the teenagers, and after a short conversation they turned and left, fencing each other with their canes and swaggering to the tunes on their ear pieces as they headed towards the city centre. The people on the wooden bridge turned and went back into the nature reserve.

"It's okay," said Judy. "I think the police got here in time. Come on kids, those ducks'll be wanting their breakfast."

The white-haired group was still there when I reached the footpath to the flats. They were muttering angrily. As I walked past one of them said, "And anyhow, who in our neighbourhood would give them any support! I don't believe it!"

And a man's deep voice responded, "If there is anyone helping them, we have a right to know! It's our park those scroungers are polluting!"

My heart was pounding hard as I typed in the code to my entrance and walked up the stairs.

Before I do anything else I need to repeat the exercise of yesterday morning. As soon as I got in I pulled my chair up to the window, and tried to focus my mind. One of the positive legacies of my earlier mainstream religious involvement is that I was given this huge knowledge of Christian writings, and although I have left a lot of the doctrine behind, the spirit of it is with me as strongly as ever. I have an ancient book of daily readings which I bought second-hand in the shop several years ago. It says in the front that it was first published in 1794 although my copy is much more recent. The price on the paper cover is in decimal sterling, so I think it must date from the time we were in the European Union, before the New Alliance. I turned to the readings for 17th October. There is always a theme, with verses taken from the old and new testaments loosely connected with that one central idea. The theme yesterday was rejoicing. The verses are quoted in a really ancient form, and it can take some time to unravel them. Sometimes I look them up in a more modern version, although I am rather out of touch with trendy translations, since the Bible does not have such a prominent place in our worship. There was a quotation from Isaiah:

"They will say of me, 'In the Lord alone
are deliverance and strength.'
All who have raged against him
will come to him and be put to shame.

But all the descendants of Israel
will find deliverance in the Lord
and will make their boast in him."

This sort of stuff can seem pretty obscure, but I have noticed that sometimes, like poetry I don't fully understand, it can bring me a huge sense of comfort or peace. I understood from these verses that people might be aggressive towards values of truth and love now, but the time will come when they will understand and feel shame. I think the 'descendants of Israel' are all those who follow the Light, and that in some way, I don't know how, we will find ways out of our difficulties by embracing that Light. I sat by the window thinking about these old verses. I started wondering about the person who had written them all those thousands of years ago. What was happening in his life? How did he still his soul, and become so open that this great optimism and faith flooded into his spirit? Gradually that gentle feeling I associate with sitting in silence with others started to creep over me. It is hard to explain. It is like waking up slowly in the morning between clean sheets, feeling rested. Or it is like stroking soft, smooth skin. It is like the first cup of coffee of the day, looking out over the sea at dawn. It is a feeling without time and without thought. It is the wind gliding between the trees.

I sat there for nearly an hour, and then I stretched and went into the kitchen to prepare my lunch. There is a peace which passes all understanding, and I would be a fool to try to understand it or how it came to me yesterday, when I started with my heart pounding and such a sense of threat. I plan to sit here again today and to be still and cool in my own mind and spirit and, if I can't experience the same thing today, at least to remember it, and to hold on to the truth of it. Then I think I will have a busy day.

Sabina and Jo are teaching this afternoon. Very occasionally I wish I had a car, because I really want to talk to one or other of them this morning, to make sure they've seen the newspaper coverage and to discuss what they might do if there are angry residents around, as there were yesterday. I don't feel comfortable about using my phone. I could catch a bus out to Jo's quite easily, but it would be time consuming, and part of me feels, after yesterday's experiences, that I should just calmly follow my usual routines, which means cleaning the flat. Actually, now I think about it I remember that I spilt gravy on the kitchen floor yesterday evening, and there was a lot of dust on my books when I picked up that little booklet of daily readings after Meeting, so it would be a good idea to have a domesticated morning. I am working in the shop this afternoon, and I need to catch up with my electronic mail tonight. The confirmation of my visa-waiver should have come through, ready for my Texas visit. I wonder how Simon is doing. Perhaps I should write to him tonight, although I haven't had a reply to my last letter yet.

Tuesday 19th October

I do love Sabina and Jo! I sat for about half an hour after writing yesterday's journal entry. I didn't have the same experience as on Sunday, I think I didn't really expect to, but I did feel a sense of non-specific well-being and a sort of quietness. Then I got up, expecting to hoover and dust, when the front door buzzer went and it was Sabina, on the intercom, waiting downstairs. She said, "I've brought Yasmin to show you her new tooth, and Jo, to have some coffee. Can we come in?"

We talked for about an hour. We agreed that as far as possible we should continue with the school exactly as normal. Jo and Fran had discussed the situation with Johnny after Second Meeting, and they had some ideas about where to park (by the rugby club) so that my angry neighbours would not see them walking across the grass. Imran took Yasmin to the park yesterday afternoon and said that by then the police had gone and the camp looked quite normal, with smoke from the camp fire, and the sounds of children playing. The trouble yesterday morning might turn out to have been nothing at all, although I think all three of us felt anxious still, and Jo told me that she and Fran have agreed with their husbands that it is better never to talk about the school in front of their children. If the children don't know anything, they can't let anything slip by accident. Then they left and I finished cleaning the flat, listening to my Arab music which suited my sense of hope and purpose.

The shop was good too. Quite a lot of people came in, and between serving them we unpacked loads of Fair Trade coffee and tea, which sells well alongside the second hand clothes! I spent the evening reading the book by Hudson and Felix about life in Kent at the beginning of this century (*Jam Tarts and Cuckoos*) for the next reading group. It is very funny, but rather cynical.

Today should be a pleasant day. The flat is looking good, and I feel quite calm about Simon and about the school. We will plan and knit this afternoon, and I will find out how Sabina and Jo got on yesterday.

Wednesday 20th October

I don't seem able to hold on to my peace of mind for more than a few days at a time just now. Yesterday started well, but our discussion over the planning and knitting left me anxious, and I woke early today with a heavy heart. I decided to sit and watch the garden and drink my coffee as the sun rose, which is around 7.30am at this time of year, but it is a cool, drizzly day and although everything gradually became lighter, the world seemed grey and brown, and not very beautiful.

Jo and Sabina had a good time with the children and the seventh and last of them came to class, which pleased them enormously. Charlie is a little girl of about six, who spends part of her time with her parents at the camp, and a few nights a week with her grandparents in Southampton. It is one of those sad situations where the grandparents don't approve of the son and daughter-in-law, and refuse point blank to help them, but they try to help their grandchild. Of course, Sabina only heard it from Charlie's mother's point of view. The chances are it looks quite different if you are one of the grandparents. Apparently Alfred was on form yesterday too, and he has started teaching Trent the banjo. There are a couple more tents over there, I'm told, and also two vans. They must drive them across the grass, which could cause some local anger if they damage the football pitches.

The part of our discussions which worried me, however, came when Jo mentioned that someone at the rugby club seemed to be checking on the cars parked on the gravel, when Jo and Sabina headed home afterwards. It's a strange area of land over there. The rugby club building is a temporary looking wooden hut with windows at one end, standing off the ground on a concrete platform, like a temporary classroom following floods. There are changing rooms, which must have no outside light, and a bar. The windows look out from the bar at the road along the front. The rugby pitches are one side of the clubhouse, upriver from it, and on the downriver side there is the gravelled area where Jo and Sabina had parked. I have walked along there quite often, and I'm fairly certain there are no signs limiting parking to club members. In fact, a couple of years ago when there was a hot air balloon festival in August I remember that area was packed with cars. I have seen dog walkers park there too.

We agreed that there could be all sorts of reasons why someone might note down car numbers: maybe they are keeping an eye out for a stolen vehicle, or they might be having issues with neighbourhood parking. The trouble is, of course, that we don't know. Still, the man didn't say anything to them, and Jo reckoned they must have looked like a couple of ordinary women and a baby who had been walking in the park on an autumn afternoon. I hope so.

My problem at the moment is that if I start worrying, the worry seems to spread to all sorts of other topics too. I have got my visa-waiver documents to visit Texas and my flights and hotels are booked, and I have the permission from the prison governor to attend Simon's execution. There have been no unusual delays, no hitches of any sort, in fact. Yet once I had started worrying about the school, or rather, about possible neighbourhood opposition to the school, the worry extended to my January visit too. I found myself replaying the interview I had at immigration two years ago, the questions they asked and the answers I gave, which were all typed into their computer. At the time I couldn't decide whether the officer was trying to catch me out, or whether he just wasn't concentrating. I remember he asked, "Are you meeting up with anybody?" and I had explained that I was over for just a week, to visit in prison. I had my itinerary on the desk, showing exactly what I was planning to do each day. Yet a couple of questions later he asked, "When did you say you are meeting your friends?" Each time when I answered he typed something onto his computer. He asked me a lot of questions about firearms too, but I have never carried or owned a gun in my life. Of course I am doing nothing illegal. I wonder, really, whether I have just read too much on the internet and heard too much discussion on television, and developed a tendency to believe conspiracy theorists when they argue that governments are trying to control us, and to invade our privacy. But, well, Karl's warnings to me seem to suggest that too, and surely a member of the ATTF would know better than anyone what is really going on?

I suppose I went to bed thinking about all this, and I seemed to dream all night, one of those monotonous dreams where the same thing keeps happening all the time. I was arguing with an official about some documents. We were in an office, it wasn't immigration it was more like the rugby club, and the official was sometimes dressed as an old fashioned British police officer with one of those high helmets, but in green, and sometimes in a suit like a weather forecaster. Then I woke before it was light, and wondered whether Simon ever gets to sleep in total darkness, or whether there are always lights in his cell and in the corridor.

Today is going to be a busy day. I am in the shop for an hour or so this morning, then Meeting for Worship, and school this afternoon. It will be good for me to get on with something constructive, instead of sitting here looking at a dull, wet garden and feeling low!

Thursday 21st October

Something very odd happened yesterday. I had quite a good time in the shop in the morning. The student Rolf was working with me and we talked more seriously this morning. He told me that his mother was a teacher, one of the many who left following the New Alliance, when the History and Science syllabuses changed so radically. Rolf is studying art at the college here, and has been doing quite well, but over some sorting-out of a huge bundle of odd socks he told me that he has started to have problems recently. "I went down to the Food Station," he explained, "and did some sketches of the people there. I asked them first. But my tutor doesn't like them. She says they are too naturalistic, with an emotional edge to them. She has banned them from being included in my second year show, and without them I don't have enough work. And if my show isn't up to scratch I can't stay on for my final year."

"Can't you get a second opinion?" It seemed a bit unfair to me. It was a whole term's work.

"Possibly," said Rolf, "but I'm not sure I want to. I might go back to London and help Mum on one of her projects." It seems Rolf's mother writes books to help children in alternative schools to learn to read. "More useful," added Rolf.

Then I went on to the Meeting House.

Sunday meetings take place in the hall opposite the original Meeting House, close to the children's playground, but Wednesday meetings did not grow when the Sunday ones did, and we have always held them in the Old Meeting Room. Paddy and I tend to take it in turns to get there early, to check everything is ready (Wednesday can be a desperately busy day for the warden) and then to settle down and establish the quietness in a house which, though not noisy, can be surprisingly busy during the week. It was my turn to be early but actually Paddy came in almost immediately after me, we seated ourselves and Paddy closed his eyes. I spent the first ten minutes or so looking at the chrysanthemums and thinking about Rolf and his mother, holding them up to the Light and feeling encouraged that there are people like that right across the country. Several people came in during that time: regulars like Leicester and Kat, and the Spanish friend of someone who goes to the evening meetings. Then I closed my eyes and tried to open my mind and heart, letting thoughts and ideas pass through my mind like the Spirit on the surface of the earth on the first day of creation. I was vaguely aware that some other people came in, and that there was a little whispering, but I was comfortably occupied and I didn't look to see who else had arrived. The half hour passed really quickly, and then Leicester was tapping my arm to indicate that Meeting was over. That was when I saw him.

It was green-jacket man. He was sitting right opposite me in the circle, his woolly hat still on his head and a grey scarf wrapped round his neck. On his lap was a copy of a leaflet someone prepared for newcomers years ago, and he was holding hands with the warden on one side and Kat on the other, according to our tradition at the end of a meeting.

I felt myself go cold. Had he followed me here? Was he spying on us all?

Paddy gave out some notices and a few people contributed comments about one thing or another. Leicester had seen an eviction taking place just down the road on his way to Meeting, and was very upset. The warden reported that a record number of people had asked to doss at the Meeting House in the last week. Then, as always, we were all invited to stay for a light lunch.

I have stopped eating the lunch since we started the school. I miss it really, the conversation, the friendliness and the warmth, but I hate to feel I'm rushing from one place to another and only just getting anywhere on time. I was wondering whether to say anything to the man, or just to leave, when he walked across the circle and held out his hand.

"Hi," he said. "I'm Derek. We meet again!"

I was not sure how to respond. "Indeed we do," I agreed. "Is this your first time at one of our meetings?"

The man seemed very relaxed, and quite well spoken. He looked rough but his accent didn't fit. He sounded as if he might have been part American, part upper-class English.

"Well, yes and no," he said. "We were all taken to a meeting when I was a teenager, along with visiting a couple of other churches, and I've always had it in my mind that I might try it again some time. After I saw you talking to that Feeding Station lady someone told me about this group, and here I am! But I thought you were a much bigger group, from what people said."

Something about Derek jarred on me. Standing there talking to him, I couldn't work out what it was, but I felt very uncomfortable, as if I were being inappropriately touched.

Kat had joined us. "This group, the Wednesday group, is small," she explained, "if you want numbers, come on Sunday! Are you local?"

"Just moved into the area," explained Derek. "I was working for Gould and Brothers, who own the 99 cent shops, but I was in their Reading branch. They offered me an assistant manager's post here. I came down two weeks ago."

"Who's the Feeding Station woman?" Kat asked.

Derek looked surprised. "I thought she came here too?" he commented.

"Sometimes," I agreed, then added for Kat, "Sky is the main

organiser of the Feeding Station by the bridge, the one in the white building. She used to come here quite regularly a few years ago and she still comes to the early meeting sometimes. She and I have been friends for years." Then I asked Derek, "If you've got a job, assistant manager, what were you doing at the Feeding Station?"

"Oh, I haven't been there!" he said, seeming surprised. "Your friend Sky came to the 99 cent store looking for stuff that was past its sell-by date. Of course, we don't give anything away. We sell it off half price just before the shop closes at nine, so she didn't get anything from us! Still," he added, changing his tone in a slightly odd way, "it was good to meet her."

"Come and have lunch," Kat suggested. Then, "Are you off now?" she asked me. I agreed, hoping Kat wouldn't mention the school, and left promptly.

Sitting here on a clear morning looking out at the garden, I am trying to understand what it was about that encounter, about both the encounters I've had with this man, which make me feel so uncomfortable, and I can't put my finger on it. It could be the way his appearance doesn't match his voice, and neither his appearance nor his voice match his job. It could be the way he said, "She didn't get anything from us!" or the way, on our first encounter, he had said, "Planning the revolution?" In both cases he seemed to be mocking us, as if he thinks that our activities are childish or insignificant. Yet he chose to come to our meeting, and you would think he would know that, if nothing else, we are deeply, some might say hopelessly, idealistic! Then there is the fact that he said he had met Sky, but Sky had no idea who he was. Sky is not like me, I find it really hard to remember faces. She would have known, surely, if she had asked him for donations and he had turned her down?

I have to be so careful, though. No human is perfect, and if I feel wary of people's foibles they will, eventually, pick it up. I don't want to be the cause of someone not feeling welcome among us, because of my unbridled suspicions.

Well, I will just hold the man, Derek, to the Light, along with all the other things that are on my mind. I want to use my morning constructively. Jo and I want to make a mobile with the children this afternoon, of water fowl, so I need to find card, thread and my rarely used chopsticks, and plan how to do it. It is a lovely, brisk autumn morning. If the weather stays like this we will be able to work round the camp fire, which gives us more space and better light than when we're in the tent. I think I will listen to something uplifting while I work.

Saturday 23rd October

It is two days since I wrote this journal, and I am still shocked and, I'll be honest, a little confused about what has happened in that time.

I was just preparing my lesson, around 10.30am on Thursday, when Kat rang up. I don't really know Kat particularly well and I can't remember her ever phoning me before, so I was surprised. She sounded stressed.

"I've been talking to Gerry," she said. Gerry is her husband. "Something happened yesterday. I think it was my fault. I'm really sorry. I hope I haven't made trouble for you."

My neck suddenly seemed stiff. "What happened yesterday?"

"Well, it might be nothing. It probably is. But Gerry said I should at least warn you. I've been worrying about it all night."

I could feel my anxious impatience growing. "What happened, Kat? What do you need to warn me about?"

"Oh, I am sorry!" Kat sounded really upset. "People keep saying that we need to be careful who we talk to, what we say in public meetings, but he seemed so interested in it, so over lunch I told him all about the school. I could see that the others were giving me funny looks but I didn't think … he asked lots of questions and he seemed so, oh, I don't know, approving!"

"Kat," I said, with a cold feeling creeping up my spine. "Who did you tell all about the school?"

"The new guy. That nice man from the 99 cents store. Derek. I told him."

"Oh, Kat!" I didn't know what to say.

Kat rushed on, "But I think he's really nice! I think he might volunteer to help. After all, you can't do everything on your own! But Gerry said I ought to warn you."

"Yes," I agreed. "Thank you. Thank Gerry too, will you." And I put the DeV phone down. It wasn't very polite but I wanted to think.

The DeV phone had been charging in the kitchen, and I was still standing there by the back door, which I rarely use, looking out through the kitchen window. The door leads out to a small platform and the fire escape. I turned to put the phone on the counter and I saw shapes through the crinkled glass. Someone was standing there. I had hardly taken it in when whoever it was knocked loudly on the glass.

The only people who come up that way are the Eastern Europeans who do the garden. It's ridiculous, but I thought it was going to be them. I knew it wasn't really, the shapes and colours disguised by the rippling glass were all wrong, but I was feeling a bit disconnected because of Kat's call. I opened the door.

Two police officers walked in. There was a time when police officers were well respected by people like me. I know that in inner cities, even in those days, they were often treated with mistrust, but my dealings with them had only ever been positive, to do with vandalism in the street, an attempted break-in once, and of course the fabulous job they did with crowd control during the coronation. Since the New Alliance, and the tendency to train our police abroad, all that has changed. When those two walked into my kitchen it felt like an aggressive act. I backed into the corner by the cooker.

"Good morning, Ma'am." There we are, clear signs of police training from across the Atlantic. Who calls people like me 'ma'am' over here? "Can we have a few words with you?" They both flashed cards at me, I suppose ID cards but to be honest I was too stunned to look properly.

"Er... come in," I said (although they already had) and I led them into the living room.

One officer, taller and thinner than the one who had so far

spoken to me, sat down on the armchair by the sideboard. The fatter one walked over to the window.

"Nice flat," he said. "Nice view. I dare say you will soon be able to see right across the park to the river, when the last of the leaves have dropped. Very scenic."

"Yes," What was he getting at?

"Of course, your view will be a bit blighted this year," he added, turning to look at me. "Oh, please sit down! We just want to have a little talk."

Of course I had no choice. I sat. My heart was pounding.

"Yes," continued the policeman. "All sorts of people in the park this autumn. Camping. Making fires. Littering the place so that ordinary people don't like to go over there. It's caused us a lot of trouble, hasn't it James?"

"Oh yes," responded the other officer, hitching up the knee of his trousers as he crossed his legs. "Yes, a lot of trouble. We would hate to think anyone might encourage them. Show too much sympathy."

The fatter policeman walked across to the settee and sat down. He leaned forward, resting his hands on his knees. "The thing is," he said, "we've had complaints."

"Complaints?" I felt stupid. "I haven't complained about anything."

"Oh no, you haven't!" said the first officer. "You haven't complained at all. It seems that you really like your new neighbours. Isn't that how it seems to us, James? Very fond of them, you seem to be."

"That's right," agreed James. "Very fond of them. We've heard all sorts of things."

"Visiting them at all hours of the day and night. Taking them gifts. Teaching the children. Oh yes, you definitely seem very enamoured with those people."

"Of course," added James, "it's a free country. She can be friends with whoever she likes."

"Oh, indeed, James. Indeed," agreed the fat officer. They were playing a game. "We can all be friends with whoever we choose, but sometimes we do bring trouble on ourselves, wouldn't you say?"

James agreed, "Oh yes, lots of trouble!"

"Neighbours could get very upset if they thought you were encouraging anti-social behaviour. They might complain to all sorts of people: city councillors, their member of parliament, even the chief constable. After all, they elected him to stand up for their rights."

"It could become very unpleasant," confirmed James.

"Oh, very unpleasant. We might even have to rehouse you. For your own good, of course."

"Oh yes, of course for your own good. You would perhaps feel happier among others who see the world as you do?"

"Who enjoy the company of losers," added the fat officer.

My mouth was dry. I was being threatened. Could they really do that, turn me out of a flat I owned?

"So what do you say?" asked the first officer. "Do you think you might choose to make some new friends? Perhaps leave that riff-raff (with a nod of his head towards the park) to us? Work a few more hours in that shop, perhaps? Knit a few more squares?"

I was stunned. I had no idea how to answer. I felt as if my face had gone very red, and the palms of my hands were sweating. I don't know what I would have said. I might have given in. I was really frightened, to be honest.

But then the doorbell rang.

It is an odd thing about the doorbells to these flats. Nobody can get into the building unless they know the code or unless they have been buzzed in after talking on the intercom, so the only people who normally ring the door bells are other residents. I thought it might be Judy.

"Excuse me," I said, and walked to the front door, feeling quite shaky. I opened the door.

"Hi!" said Karl, smiling, taking his cap off and holding it in his hand. "Are you ready?"

I couldn't think what he was talking about. He winked at me as he had that time in Reception at school, then sauntered into the living room.

He looked genuinely surprised. "Good heavens!" he exclaimed and then turned with a look of great concern on his face. "Are you all right? What's happened?"

I had followed him into the room. He turned and put an arm protectively around me. "What's going on?"

The two police officers jumped to their feet. The one called James had a look of utter confusion on his face, the fatter one looked a bit angry. They were both, of course, outranked by Karl. They would have been outranked by him even if Karl hadn't been an officer. The ATTF has a lot of power.

"Officers," said Karl, holding out his arm to shake hands. "Please, tell me what has happened."

"Oh, ah, nothing," said the fatter policeman. "We came here just to warn your … to warn her, we've had some trouble in the neighbourhood!"

"Really?" Karl sounded surprised. "In this neighbourhood? It always seemed so quiet to us."

By now, of course, I knew that the policemen weren't the only ones to be playing games. Karl still had his arm round my shoulder, which he very rarely does. He didn't sound like the Karl I know either, more formal, older maybe. It was clear that the policemen were stumped, though.

Karl went on, "So what's happened? Anything I can help you with? I'm often here, you know."

Now that was an outright lie. Karl has been to my flat to pick me up quite frequently, and he has helped now and again with technical things like connecting up my DeV47 to my TV screen and my phone when the systems were integrated, but he's only eaten here a couple of times and never stayed overnight. Still, the message to the officers must have come over loud and clear. If they messed with me, they would be messing with him too.

"Oh, no, not these flats," the fatter officer was almost falling over his own words, trying to extricate himself from the situation in which he had suddenly found himself. "Just some trouble …"

"Across the park," James chipped in, trying to help. "In the encampment."

Karl allowed his face to light up. He withdrew his arm from my shoulder and sauntered across to the window. "Oh, I see!" he said, looking very relaxed. "Well, I'm sure you don't need to worry about that!" Then, looking at me he added, "We're on very good terms with the tent dwellers, aren't we?"

I swallowed. What was Karl playing at?

"Of course, I don't suppose ordinary officers, a constable and a sergeant I see, would be given this sort of information, but decisions have been made. To stop the human rights lobby from protesting too much, you understand? There's actually a little informal school over there now, you know. I'm sure the good people of this neighbourhood won't have any trouble." Then a frown appeared on Karl's forehead. "Unless the people here are causing difficulties? People can be very short-sighted, I've noticed, when it comes to keeping an eye on their own area."

"Oh, I'm sure that won't happen. I mean, I don't think anyone round here will make trouble!" stuttered Officer One.

"No, no!" James agreed. "Absolutely! That's what we wanted to say! Best to leave the people in the park alone! Live and let live!"

"Quite," said Karl. "Well, thank you for dropping by. I'm sure you have many other people to visit. Let me see you to the door." And he ushered them out, looking relaxed and benign. I sat back hard on my arm chair and gulped. Karl had rescued me, that was obvious, but how had he known? What was going on?

He explained it over dinner.

We were sitting in his flat. He had picked me up after my lesson and we drove over to his place, hardly speaking. I felt like a naughty child. I wished I had told him about the school, but I've hardly seen him recently and anyhow, I knew he wouldn't approve. Karl had a couple of brown paper sacks on the back seat, with a bottle of wine sticking out of one. "Italian food, tonight!" he announced as we carried them into his flat.

It wasn't until the food was cooking, delicious smells wafting through from the kitchen, that Karl poured me a gin and tonic and asked, "So how did it go this afternoon?"

"Good," I said, although actually I had pretty much gone through the afternoon on auto-pilot, my mind going over and over the events of the morning, my heart still pounding. "How long have you known?"

Karl sighed. "You know that …" he said. Of course I did. I've known since the first time I met Karl that somehow he knows exactly what I'm doing all the time. I thought at first it was just because he could access my DeV, but we had been really careful not to email or phone … still Karl is ATTF. If they want to know about something, then they know about it. But those police officers knew a lot too, ever such a lot…

"You're playing with fire," he said. "I suppose you know that?"

"Well, we shouldn't be!" I exclaimed, frustrated. "All we're doing is teaching a few kids who can't get places in local schools! We're hardly threatening to bring down the government, and anyhow …"

"Anyhow, maybe they should be brought down?" queried Karl. "That is what you think, isn't it?"

I took a deep breath. "I think," I said, "that this is supposed to be a democracy, and that means that if we don't like what one political party does, we can change it. I think that there are basic human rights. I think we are doing the right thing."

Karl was quiet for a few seconds. "The right thing," he said, thoughtfully. "Yes, but which right thing?"

"What do you mean?"

"I mean," said Karl, sounding a bit weary, "that sometimes there is more than one right thing. I agree, those children have the right to an education, in theory. But if you help those families out now, if you make it easy for them to live in the camp, you'll make it harder for them to adjust to the realities of life. People have to learn to take responsibility for themselves."

This argument always makes me fume. It is what lies behind the recent reforms, it is why so many people are homeless. It denies that we have responsibilities for each other. It refuses to accept, 'Love your neighbour as yourself.'

I didn't answer. I was thinking what a wide gap there is between Karl and me when push comes to shove.

We both sipped our gin and tonics. Karl sighed.

"Look," he said, "I know I'm not going to change you. But you've got to understand that you're dealing with some powerful forces here. If I hadn't come over this morning … "

"I know," I said, "thank you."

"That's OK. And I will go on keeping an eye on you," he said. "You can run your school, for the time being. On one condition…"

I didn't say anything. Who was Karl to offer me protection, to give me permission to do something that is perfectly legal anyhow, to set conditions?

He touched my hand briefly. "Just listen," he recommended.

"Okay."

"You believe in keeping the law, don't you?" Karl knows I do, we have discussed it before. Without the rule of law a country is lost.

"So all I want is this," he said. "If when you're over there you hear that anyone is up to no good: drugs, or theft, or anything else … um … provocative, civil disobedience maybe, you'll let me know, won't you? Nothing else, just let me know."

I thought about it. I could imagine all sorts of situations where the tent dwellers might do something that is not strictly within the law, and I would not be prepared to tell anyone.

"Perhaps," I said.

Karl sighed again. "I'll consider that a 'yes'," he said, "at least as far as my bosses are concerned." Then, rather seriously, "Don't shut me out, will you?"

I didn't answer. We were both quiet again, then he changed the subject. "Dinner in ten minutes!" he announced.

CHAPTER 3

Whenever I wrote this journal yesterday evening in the hotel, I thought I would not open it again until I reached Houston, but in fact I have travelled very little, perhaps three miles. I am sitting in Terminal Five at Heathrow, having passed without incident through check-in and security, but my plane is delayed for four hours, due to fog. I suppose there are worse places to wait. Since the New Alliance, Terminal Five has been the only terminal used for traffic between the States and England, and the tone and facilities are very American. There are lots of coffee places and doughnut outlets (written 'donut') and a slight smell of cinnamon in the air. It feels as if once I had gone through security I had already changed countries. Most of the other passengers waiting in Departure are Americans, quite a few in uniform, and just along from me there is a group of four ATTF officers, three men and a woman, looking very smart and carrying cabin luggage in the same khaki and dark blue of their uniforms. Perhaps they are issued with their luggage along with their clothing.

I have read again the posters on the walls reminding non-Americans of the terms of entry. They are exactly the same in design and content as the information I read on the internet and which arrived by registered mail a month ago, but it does no harm to be sure I have done everything as they like. I have slotted the extra pages into the back of my passport, the pages where I have had to enter any medication I have taken in the last month (because of the spot checks for drugs on entry into the USA) and the internet searches I have pursued in the same period. They can check both these things electronically, of course, so I assume that making would-be immigrants fill them in on paper documents is either a way of trying to catch us out, or a way of intimidating us. In theory, following the signing of the New Alliance, we were supposed to be on equal terms with the USA, their citizens able to come and go freely into England and Wales (not Scotland, of course, they're still in the EU), and English and Welsh people able to travel freely to the USA. The first part happened at once, although we don't see many American tourists, mostly military or political advisers and their families, but the second part, about us travelling freely, hasn't happened yet. Of course there was massive opposition to the New Alliance from some quarters, and a famous Liberal Lord staged a protest here at Terminal Five which attracted a lot of media attention, and then someone decided our passports needed to be changed before we could travel freely. I have one of the new sorts of passports, but by the time it was issued all this trouble had broken out in the Caribbean, and so that part of the treaty was delayed again. I wonder whether we will ever be given easy access into the USA. And come to think of it, I wonder if I am wise in writing this in my journal? But the USA is supposed to be a free democracy; surely however suspicious of foreigners they are, they still allow people to wonder about the future?

This visit, or rather the thought of it, has dominated everything I have done for three months, and before I left the flat yesterday with Fran, who gave me a lift, I was as nervous as if it were me who was to be executed. No, I must remember not to exaggerate. I really cannot imagine how Simon must be feeling, but definitely worse than I felt yesterday morning. The strange thing is, though, that after I wrote that extra entry into this journal last night I started to feel quite peaceful. I wish I could say that it was a peace that came from the Spirit within, and indirectly perhaps that is so, but the reality is, as I have noticed in the past, that if I am nervous or anxious about something I often feel much better once I get started on it. Fran and I had already had dinner in the hotel restaurant, so when I had written my diary and emailed Amy to say I was safely at the hotel, I made some hot chocolate and drank it in bed, watching a Japanese detective movie dubbed into American English, and then went fast asleep. It was probably the best night's sleep I've had in ages, so this morning I feel very positive, despite the departure delay.

I am going to use the time, first of all, catching up on thank-you letters for Christmas presents. I feel a bit guilty that I haven't done this sooner – I used to expect to write post-Christmas letters between Christmas Day and New Year's Day, but of course this Christmas that was impossible, what with the extended house party at Amy's and the need to plan the tent school programme for the new year. I have just bought some cards from a stationer's across from this bench, and I can post them all before I leave, as long as I can buy stamps somewhere. I have my book, too, a novel by Eugenia Markwell set in Alaska. It had excellent reviews and I downloaded it, along with various other books, onto my DeV ready for this trip. I discovered two years ago when I last visited Simon that I was bound to spend long hours in my hotel room at Stanley. There is really nothing to do in that little town, and I hate the suspicion with which I am treated every time I open my mouth and sound 'foreign'. The hotel, on the other hand, is rather friendly. Over the years they have had a lot of English and European visitors and we bring good business to a relatively poor area. In an odd sort of way their death penalty is good for tourism. I wonder if that will change if we re-introduce the death penalty here in England, as some members of the government propose?

I also plan to eat here, before boarding. We were due to leave at 11.30am, and lunch was to be served on the plane, but now I can't see us boarding before 3.00pm. I don't mind. There is a Tex-Mex restaurant down by Gate 17. I rather enjoy Tex-Mex food, and it will help to pass the time.

Sunday 9th January

I woke up at midnight last night, having gone to bed right after dinner at about 8.30pm, and then more or less on the hour until

7.00am Texas time. It was jet lag, of course. Now I am up, showered and breakfasted, and back in my room. I will not check out until I have to, at midday, and I have booked a taxi to take me all the way to Stanley. Even so, I might arrive at the hotel there before it is time to check in, because it is a good road all the way.

Yesterday was a long day. I wrote all my thank-you letters, seven in the end because I decided that as Meggan's children had each given me a present, they should each get a 'thank you'. I think they might like the novelty of receiving cards in the post too, since most kids communicate electronically all the while. I found two book stalls selling US stamps and was about to give up when I found a kiosk by the duty free selling English stamps, and so I was able to post them there. A nice thing happened, too, while I was writing the cards. The woman from the ATTF group came over to me and said, "I'm going to buy us all coffee. Would you like one?"

I was quite surprised. "Oh, thank you…" I spluttered.

"It's okay," she said. "We saw the code on your cabin luggage," (she was referring to the sticker put there when I went through security), "and we realised you're on the Houston flight, like us. I hate these delays, don't you? Would you like Americano or Cappucino?"

"Oh, Cappucino, please," I said, rooting round for my purse.

"No, it's okay," said the girl (she was a young woman really), "we're on expenses. I'll get it." And off she went.

When she returned with a tray of cardboard cups, she had doughnuts too, and it seemed unfriendly to go on writing cards, so I moved up the row to where they were sitting and we all talked over our drinks. They had seen the same Japanese movie as me, and we discussed the rather odd plot. I didn't ask them why they were heading west, and they didn't ask me. It was a friendly and pleasant interlude and afterwards I went back to writing my cards feeling generally pleased with the world. I don't know how large the ATTF is, and I wondered whether they might have met Karl at some point. One of their group was even the same rank. Somehow, though, it seemed like the sort of question one didn't ask.

We actually boarded earlier than predicted, not long after

2.00pm, and took off around 2.45pm. They did offer us the promised lunch but I had eaten chicken enchiladas (very good) so I declined, but drank a G and T and dozed for a while. The plane was only half full, and I had a window seat with two empty seats between me and the aisle. The ATTF officers travelled Business Class, but quite a few of the people in Economy were in uniform, with just a smattering, like me, in ordinary clothes. I started the Alaskan novel, which is certainly quite gripping, and listened to country music on the in-flight entertainment. They served us dinner at about 7.00pm English time, but of course that is 1.00pm Texas time so by today's standards it was lunch. I couldn't sleep, although I would have liked to because I find these eleven hour flights quite boring. I thought of writing this journal again, but having updated it at the airport there was really nothing else to say. I watched a movie set way back at the time of the Vietnam War, and a news programme which included some quite horrific coverage of the situation in the Caribbean, and then at last we were flying down almost following the Mississippi south, then over woods and lakes, and into Houston.

I am staying at the same hotel by the airport where I stayed two years ago. It is very pleasant, although the big difference is the beggars on the street by the entrance. I got a hotel car from the airport and the driver just swished past them, but I saw that private cars arriving at the hotel had to pass a phalanx of men, women and children, calling out and holding baseball caps to the closed windows of the cars, asking for donations. Inside the hotel everything is clean and fresh, with polished marble floors and deep leather sofas. The lifts are almost soundless and the corridor of Floor 8 is carpeted in deep purple, with paler lilac tones by each door. My room looks out across the clutter of concrete and glass buildings stretching towards downtown Houston. Everything looks crisp and smart, but somewhere there are the homes of all those beggars. I can't imagine what their lives might be like.

When I checked my emails before breakfast there was one from Karl. The last time I saw him was on New Year's Eve when he came over to Amy's. He told us he had come straight from work, and he

102

was in uniform. Quite a lot of Amy's guests are the sort of people who strongly approve of the ATTF, and he was surrounded by people all evening. He and I barely exchanged more than a few sentences in private, but when he left around 2.00am he said quietly to me, "I'll be thinking of you," and I felt he had forgiven me for embarking on this trip, even though he thinks it is foolhardy and can't achieve anything. The email I picked up this morning is light in tone. Of course he knows how easy electronic mail is to access, since he seems to spend his time accessing other people's, so I suppose he would be careful. He says he is just back from Milton Keynes and now has a few days off. He plans to do some cooking for his freezer, and to do some serious work in the gym. He has to be away on the twelfth and thirteenth, but should be home by the fourteenth and will pick me up from the airport on the morning of the fifteenth. I feel ridiculously pleased and grateful.

I feel the need to bring my day into the Light. I will stay in my room until just before noon, reading and maybe playing games on my DeV. I would have liked to bring some knitting to do but there is a problem with carrying knitting needles, even in the luggage that went into the hold. When I queried it, the officials said that if I wanted knitting needles I could buy then in the States, and no doubt that is true, but not at an airport hotel in Houston, and definitely not anywhere I can get to in Stanley!

Then I will go by taxi to the hotel where I stayed before, and spend the afternoon, I suppose, in my room there. The hotel has no dining facilities but there are several restaurants in its immediate vicinity, and I will eat there. Tomorrow I believe I can visit Simon all day – as long as nobody else has turned up to visit. When I enquired three months ago I was the only person requesting to witness his execution and the prison officer said they would let me know if that changed, but I don't think they would. More to the point, Simon hasn't mentioned anyone else being around. When I think about the fact that by Wednesday evening Simon will be dead it feels totally unreal, as if I were told that by Wednesday I would be in New York or Bombay. I no longer feel that turbulent anxiety that

I felt as I packed, in fact I feel like an actress in a play. It is very disconcerting.

I want to hold the tent school in the Light too. It is strange that now that the tent community has become so large, and the school is made up of three different classes, it is easier for me to be away. Sabina is brilliant with the little ones and Claire is pretty much a fully-fledged teacher now, since she started to be involved in the planning in November. The eights to elevens are the difficult ones, especially since the Hewett family arrived in late October, with their two very distressed boys. They were kept in a holding centre for a month while their parents served sentences for disturbing the peace on the day they were evicted, and although none of us knows the details, the boys seem more traumatised than you might expect if the worse that had happened is that they were separated from their parents for four weeks. The eights to elevens are my favourite group but Fran, Jo, Billy and Seb can manage perfectly well without me while I'm away. There are only two kids, still, in the senior group so I don't think there'll be any issues there. Term started last week, and there were no problems with the neighbours, so maybe that particular issue is not going to raise its head on these short, dark winter days. Let's hope so, anyhow.

I think I need to hold myself in the Light too. Despite this distant, unreal feeling I have, I know that I am a long way from home, and vulnerable.

Monday 10th January. 5.30am

I can't sleep. It's probably not surprising, what with the time difference and the day which awaits me. The best thing to do, I think, is to sit here by my darkened window and to write this journal, bringing my life and myself into the ordering of Truth.

I am still in my PJs, with a sweat shirt on top. I have made some coffee, and I'm sitting on the one armchair, in the circle of light shed by a standard lamp. I have half drawn back the curtains, not more because I know that there are little houses across on the other side of the patch of mown grass, and I don't feel like being too visible.

The taxi drive was pleasant. He was a Latino, less phased by my non-American accent than many a white driver, and we talked a little about my flight over and the hotel where I had stayed, which has a good name. He told me about his children and their reactions to their Christmas presents. He tried asking me about my children and grandchildren but when he drew a blank conversation dried up. He didn't ask me what I am doing in the States or why I wanted to go to Stanley, although he did mention that the fishing is good in the lake, if you go at the right time of the year. The journey took exactly two hours.

My room was ready when I checked in, in fact I think the hotel is half empty, and I passed the afternoon reading and watching some fairly mindless TV.

I am not at all sleepy, I can almost feel the adrenalin rushing through my veins, so it might be a good time to think about this hotel, and the people who run it. It is one of an American chain of hotels, inexpensive without being cheap in the wrong sense of the word. There is a manageress who seems very involved in every aspect of the business, and she has very good people skills. For example, she remembered me when I checked in yesterday, and it is two years or more since I was last here. Stanley is a racially mixed community. Mixed, but apparently not really integrated. Between the hotel and the prison, on the edges of the little town, there are several small black communities, each with its own wooden, white-painted church and some with a café or a little store, with faded advertisements for soft drinks and breakfast cereals. The homes are generally either small wooden houses on stilts, with rickety decks at the front (do they call them 'porches'?) or trailers, although every now and again there is a very smart brick-built bungalow. I think all the children in Stanley go to the same high school, but I once went to a church in the town and it was all white, and the hotel staff here are all white too. I wonder how this works. Does the manageress appoint her friends? They certainly seem like a close-knit team. Or is there some sort of policy passed down from a central office somewhere? Would that even be allowed? I know that twenty years ago in the UK any race discrimination was totally taboo, but that more recently, with the emphasis on choice, it has been harder for would-be employees to take employers to court, since the employers' freedom of choice is now protected. Perhaps the same thing has happened here?

There are, however, black guests. Two were checking in ahead of me when I arrived, and I saw that the manageress was as courteous and friendly to them as she was to me. She also offered my Latino driver a coffee when he carried in my suit case. Of course, the all-white employee situation might just be coincidence, but it is hard to imagine.

Across the parking lot from the hotel there are several eating places. One is a Chinese restaurant, another is the Tex-Mex place where I learnt to like that sort of food on my first visit here. I think there is a barbecue place too, but I once put my head round the door and everyone stopped talking and looked at me. There were quite a few men wearing cowboy hats, and I think they were drinking beer, and I felt it might not be a good place for me to go to on my own. It was probably me being melodramatic again. There is also a rather pleasant restaurant that only serves lunches and closes soon afterwards. Last night I ate at the Tex-Mex, and drank a glass of dark Mexican beer. I walked back in the steamy night. It can be warm in Texas even in January.

I don't know how today will work. I have booked a taxi for 7.45am, so that I should be there at the start of visiting at 8.00am. On the phone the officer I spoke to said I could visit all day until 5.00pm, but that only two people can visit at a time. I would be surprised if anyone else turns up, but Simon is about to die and who knows whether friends and relatives might make one more effort to see him? I wonder what we will talk about, and how it will be. In the past two sets of visits I have found the whole business very uncomfortable. The chairs are too low for someone my size to sit normally, hold the phone with its short flex to my ear, and see

Simon. I once knelt on the chair for greater comfort but was sharply reprimanded by the officer in charge of the visiting room. The phones are made of some cheap metal and after four hours my ears are always sore from pressing the rough edges against them. Those visits were four hours long. How will it be if I am there all day?

I feel slightly sick, but that feeling of being an actress in a play or a film is still with me too, as if this is not really me who is about to shower, dress, eat breakfast and then be driven through the green Texas forests to see a man who is about to die.

Tuesday 6th January. 5.45am

Here I am again, sitting in the glow of the standard lamp, with this journal in front of me and a Gideon Bible at my feet. I have just sat here for twenty minutes, recovering from a nightmare and trying to think about all that happened yesterday. I slept surprisingly deeply last night, but my rest was squirming with difficult dreams, and I could not surface to shake them off. I can't remember ever having such a night before, but then the circumstances are pretty unusual too.

The drive through the countryside in the early morning was pleasant. The sun rose as I was having breakfast, a faded golden glow in the east, and the sky was a pale grey-blue by the time the taxi picked me up. The driver was an elderly white guy, wearing jogging trousers and a t-shirt, with a slightly grubby white cowboy hat on the rear seat. I sat at the front, and he asked me at once where I am from. When I said, "England" he didn't look as disapproving as some, just commented that he had heard that the country was coming along well, and that the government is interested in easing up on our 'crazy' gun laws (his words, not mine). I have learnt not to get into these sorts of conversations, so I made a non-committal grunt and then asked how Stanley is faring nowadays. I had noticed that there are some new buildings alongside the loop that comes in from the Interstate. This successfully launched the driver into talk about construction workers bringing business into the town, and the community's attempts to keep young people here, rather than seeing a steady exodus to Houston each year. We drove along town roads, past restaurants, fast food outlets and a used car lot, past bail-bond offices with garish advertising outside, then into the country past the little settlements I described yesterday, past a huge prison for illegal immigrants, and then right to the unit including the death row. And all the time this strange feeling of distance, of disconnection, was with me.

The guard checked the taxi, trunk and boot, the glove compartment and under the seats, while the driver and I stood to one side. I showed my passport and recited Simon's number and there was some talk about how I was to get back. I had a card from the taxi company in my clear plastic pencil case, the only container I was allowed to take in, and then the taxi took me up to the entrance.

This prison – I suspect it is typical – was not built with the comfort or convenience of visitors in mind. Outside the main doors there is a bench seat made of concrete, which can seat maybe three adults, under a high roof covering. No visitor can enter the building until the officers open the doors at 8.00am, and if it is raining and windy visitors stand in the wet outside. On the other occasions when I have been there, there is usually a queue of visitors, usually white Europeans and black Americans, all carrying their plastic bags or pencil cases, and the change which is the only money one can take in. The black visitors are usually smartly dressed, children in pretty clothes, women with beautiful make-up. The Europeans dress casually, as indeed I had yesterday and will do today, in duller colours and natural fibres, the clothing of middle class liberals when not at work. Yesterday I was only the second person to arrive, the girl ahead of me looked either Latino or Native American I thought, I cannot really tell the difference, with hair in a plait down her back and a red knitted cardigan over crisp pale blue jeans. Right behind me came an old woman in the uniform of the Salvation Army. She smiled at the girl in front. "Maria," she said, "so you made it! Your father will be so pleased."

The feeling of being in a film, with a script already written for me, grew deeper. I felt a vague, hollow feeling and instead of thinking, "Should I introduce myself?" I found myself thinking, "What would she do now?" meaning my character in a book or a play. Then, without working out the answer I found myself saying, "Maria? Are you Simon's daughter?" and then introducing myself.

Maria, who had been sitting on the concrete bench, stood up and took a small step towards me. "Oh!" she said, "Oh! Yes! Pa said you would come ... I didn't think ... Hey, you're not at all how I pictured you. Oh ... thank you." Then, to the Salvation Army woman, "This is my Pa's English pen friend."

Some more visitors arrived, dropped off by a huge SUV with 'Don't mess with Texas' on the rear bumper. Then some others walked across the car park.

Maria seemed more in control of herself than I was. She turned back to me and said, "I'm the only one visiting from Corpus Christi, so I think it'll be just you and me. We can go in together if you want?"

I was a bit concerned. "But don't you want time on your own with your father? I can wait out here."

"No!" Maria's tone was almost scornful. "It's easier with someone else there, and Pa will be so pleased to see you. Anyway, I guess it's going to be a long day!"

Just then the officers opened the doors and the process of passing through the metal detector, answering questions, being patted down and handing over IDs took over. When about five of us had been given numbers on yellow plastic plates to wear on chains round our necks, they opened the first of the electric doors, and we started the walk to the visitors' room.

I have only been to one prison in England, and that was years ago, when I was still into more conventional religion and we were invited to take a Christmas service. The building was old – probably Victorian. I don't remember much about the security but I'm pretty sure that once we were in we stayed inside, walking along corridors and through doors which were opened and closed by an officer with a bunch of keys. Simon's prison isn't like that. We passed through two electrically operated doors, across an open expanse of beautifully but rather unimaginatively kept garden, then into another building with shiny floors to rival the marble flooring of the airport hotel in Houston, through more electric doors and into a space with scratched plastic-looking windows, vending machines, and rows of cages where the prisoners are contained while they see their visitors. Tantalisingly, there are also wooden picnic tables in an area which is more airy, open on one side to the gardens, but those places are for prisoners not on death row, who must receive their visitors at different times, though I can't imagine when.

In the visitors' room we had to hand over dockets and be allocated a cage. When the officer saw the paperwork Maria and I had been given, she looked bothered.

"You can't visit this prisoner today! They shouldn't have let you in." Then, grumpily to herself, "Don't they ever think up there?"

I have a theory that something always goes wrong when visiting on death row. At less stressed times than this I have even played a guessing game with myself (and once with a German woman I met who was also visiting) about what could go wrong this time. Nevertheless, I felt a sort of lurching feeling in my stomach. Maria, who has beautiful olive coloured skin, seemed to go a deeper tan. "Keep cool!" I admonished myself, and said to the officer, "These visits were arranged before I left England. I spoke to the Warden's secretary …"

The officer muttered some more. "Wait here!" she instructed and started allocating booths to the Europeans who had come in behind us. Only when there were no other people demanding her attention did she turn back to us.

"You'd have to see him over there," the officer pointed to a cage apart from the others, where two suited men were consulting deeply over a pile of papers, "and that room's in use all day."

Maria looked really upset. "But my pa's going to die on Wednesday and I've come from Corpus Christi, and this lady's come from England …"

110

The officer muttered again under her breath. Prisoners had started to be brought down from the cells, each handcuffed and accompanied by three officers, and deposited in the cages to begin their visits. An announcement was made over the loud speaker system, and then repeated. The suited men continued to consult without looking up. I still felt like a character in a play, as if I were watching all this from the outside. I think the officer wanted us to give up and leave but there was no way either Maria or I were going to do that. We both just stood there. Finally the officer sighed, picked up the phone, told us, "Wait over there," and turned her back on us. She talked, quietly and angrily, and then slammed the phone down. She walked across to the two guys, and said something to them. One of them looked at his watch and shrugged, the other started packing up the papers, and the officer came back to us, still frowning.

"All right," she muttered. "You can have your visit!" It couldn't have been done with worse grace.

In fact the day passed more easily than I dared hope. Maria was right, it was very much easier with two people. She is a lively conversationalist. She was very funny when she talked about the teachers in her high school, and her description of her Social Studies class was particularly sharp. I could see that Simon adores her. Maria's stories reminded me of things that had happened when I was teaching, and that started me off too, then they both asked me questions about England and it all became quite lively. Our conversation totally ignored the reason we were there. We bought Simon some food from the vending machines, delivered by the officer who was now rather more friendly, and ate a light (and rather unpleasant) lunch ourselves from the same source. At some point someone turned on the overhead neon lights, and in no time at all a different officer (they had changed shifts) was tapping me on the shoulder and saying, "Five more minutes" and we were exchanging the usual comments like, "Be good!" and "See you tomorrow". I no longer felt like an actress. Something about the time we had all spent together, and especially the laughter, had brought me back to a sense of wholeness, and I didn't even feel jet lagged. We walked out into a gloomy, damp early evening, feeling stiff and tired, and Maria offered me a lift back to my hotel in her hired car. She is staying in a cheap motel on the edge of town.

If that had been it for the day I might have slept better last night, but we had a conversation in the car which has left me feeling really confused. As we left the guard post on our way out I said, "I'm glad you were able to come, I can see how much Simon cares for you," and Maria replied, "Yes, well, I never wanted to stop visiting, but he was so upset with me, trying to tell me what to do, not to go out with foreigners. I didn't know how to deal with him."

I wasn't sure how much to divulge of what Simon had written to me. "Was that the problem, then?" I asked.

"Well, to be fair … he is English like you, so only just foreign, but he's way older than me."

"I think no man is ever good enough for a girl's father," I suggested. "How much older than you is he?"

"Karl?" she said. "I don't know. He's like, your age. But he's really cool."

I felt a sort of lurch. An Englishman about my age called Karl? "What does he do?" I asked, trying to sound as casual as I could.

"Oh, law enforcement back in England. He comes over for training, like a lot of your cops do. Weapons training."

"Where does he live … in England I mean. Do you know?"

"Of course," giggled Maria, looking younger than seventeen. "We usually email but I got his address to send him a valentine's day card. He lives in some place called Milton Keynes."

Wednesday 12th January. 5.05am

All things considered, it's not surprising I'm finding it difficult to settle in the Light this morning and to find a still core of peace. There seems to be nothing at all peaceful in my life. There must be hundreds of Karls in England around my age. It's a name, like my name, common to a particular age group and rarely given to babies nowadays. In fact, I worked with a Karl, and there were three Karls in my previous church, although that was unusual. I also know that our police numbers have increased significantly with the protests following the New Alliance and the benefit reforms, and very few were weapon trained until recently. Now, of course, they all are. All of which means that I am being silly, even neurotic, linking Maria's Karl with mine. Mine? Of course, he isn't that, either.

I think the thing that should be most on my mind today, and in a way is, is the event I am going to witness this afternoon. When we had finished our visit yesterday Maria and I sat in the car in the prison car park and cried until an officer in a Stetson came over and moved us on. I don't know what to expect of myself, although I have been told what to expect of the procedure. I'm dreading it.

And as if that were not enough, I decided to check my emails just before I went to bed last night, and there is one from Jo. It is sensibly non-committal. Knowledge of the tent school is no longer secret, but we have more or less maintained our ban on communicating about it electronically. Jo tells me that 'all our projects' are going well and that my friends send their love. Then she says, 'By the way, you might be interested to know that Derek has asked to be interviewed for membership.' Derek is green-jacket man. He has been coming to Meeting more or less regularly since October and some people think he is really great. For some reason I just don't trust him at all. Whenever we speak I feel as if I am talking to a shadow or a cardboard cut-out. If he is accepted into membership he will be able to come to all our Business Meetings. There will be no secrets from him at all, and I dread to think what he might do with the information he gleans.

Yesterday was actually a good day. Maria picked me up about 7.30am. I was already waiting on the seat outside the main hotel entrance, where the smokers sit, and Maria had the car lights on because it was such a gloomy morning. We drove in silence until we got to the left turn by the high school, then Maria started talking about her childhood. She just launched in, saying, "He used to meet me from school on Fridays, when I was in elementary school. He finished work early for the weekend and we used to go to the ice cream parlour. You know, when you're a kid you think your pa will always be there."

"Yes." What could I say?

"I just can't believe … I sort of thought I'd get a call from Ma today saying he'd got a stay. She promised to keep her DeV and her TV on. But no, there haven't been any changes. Ma just texted 'Thinking of you all'. Did you sleep last night?"

"Yes, but with nightmares," I replied and then we were quiet again.

Simon, however, was not quiet. I suspect he had decided to do everything in his power to make the day as easy as possible. He had written some words on his white jumpsuit, prompts for different topics of conversation, it turned out, and if we started to get sad or we veered too close to a painful subject, he turned the talk to something new. Maria and I quickly caught on, and we did the same. One of Simon's topics was English Pubs, which are completely different from American bars. I pretended we three were sitting together in the Old Oak at the end of the road where I used to live, instead of talking over distorting metal phones through bullet proof glass. I described what we could see around us, and suggested what the other customers were like. We decided we would have lunch so I made up a menu and we each ordered. Simon wanted traditional fish and chips, once I had explained what it was, Maria decided on a steak and ale pie, and I chose liver and bacon with mashed potatoes (a meal which the other two thought sounded horrible. I think they don't eat offal). One of the officers came along to tell Simon something, and Simon told him what we were doing, and the officer said he would have fish and chips with Simon, and did we still wrap them up in newspaper as they did in the old black and white films? I think the officers are being rather nice to Simon now, and also to Maria and me. We were treated really courteously as we went through security in the morning, very different from Monday

The only really sad moments came at the end of the afternoon.

A prison chaplain dropped by, and told Maria and me a little about how today was likely to pan out. We can visit until 12 noon, then Simon will be taken by road to Chasserton, where there is an older prison and a huge graveyard, and where they still perform the executions. We have to make our own way there, of course, and the chaplain advised us to go first to some house run by a religious group which favours the death penalty, but which supports the friends and relatives as an act of Christian charity. I wonder how I feel about being the recipient of Christian charity (it sounds like something Victorian, the Poor Law or something like that) but I am glad that there will be others around to help Maria. I am way outside my comfort zone, and only just coping. My legs feel weak and my heart keeps giving little flutters.

We ate together in the evening, at a Buffalo Steak House near Maria's motel. It was quite pleasant, with pine tables and high school girls as waitresses wearing red and white striped aprons over jeans and t-shirts. We talked about Maria's childhood, and about the night Simon was arrested, and Maria got angry about her mother, who she feels has not been supportive. "Pa was a good husband to her, I would have thought she might stand by him," she exclaimed.

I told Maria I once read a book about the strain on relatives of having someone on death row, but she just commented, "I suppose so," and sort of hunched over her burger. After all, she is only seventeen. A bit of attitude is to be expected.

Then back to my hotel, and when I checked my emails there were dozens of messages from home, from people in Meeting, from Sabina and Imran, and a lovely long email from Amy saying, among other things, that the thank-you cards I had posted at the airport had arrived and that the children were thrilled to receive mail of their own. There was a one-liner from Karl, 'Thinking of you', and I wondered who else he might be thinking of, then told myself off for being ridiculous.

So now, here we are. The day has come. Somewhere there is peace. Somewhere there is Truth, and Mercy, and Kindness, but I can't access those things. In me there is just adrenalin, a pounding heart, a sick feeling, and some deep, half-hidden anger. I lift my weakness to the Light and ask for strength from outside myself. I have none within.

Thursday 13th January 8.00am

If I slept at all last night it was only for very short periods, and lightly. Now I am sitting in my hotel room looking out at the little bungalows across the mown grass, where lights are coming on and someone has just put a bag of something into a car, and although I know it is Thursday, and I know just where I am, the events of yesterday seem to overlay everything else, as if they are more real than the real world. I went to breakfast later than usual this morning, there is no hurry today, nobody to visit. I sat with a paper plate of scrambled eggs in front of me and then the television, which is always on in the lobby, started to announce that yesterday at 6.11pm Simon McKellar was pronounced dead in the execution chamber at Chasserton. Suddenly I was there, standing next to Maria (they provide no seats for friends or family, you have to stand to watch the person you love being murdered) and we were holding hands, and Maria was sobbing and trying not to. I felt a sort of rushing in my head, it's difficult to describe, and I knew that if I ate anything I would be sick. It would have been like eating while the drugs ran into Simon's veins. I threw the plate of eggs into the bin and left the lobby. When I got back to this room my head was pounding and I felt close to fainting. I lay on my unmade bed until it wore off a bit, but I am still shaky. Gradually, as I write this, the scene of Simon's execution is fading a little and the chair on which I'm sitting now seems more real, as if the present is coming into focus again.

If I write about yesterday, will the same thing happen again? But if this journal means anything, I need to record the day. I have three hours. Maria is picking me up for coffee at eleven, and then we will drive over to Chasserton to talk about the cremation.

When we arrived at the prison yesterday the chaplain was sitting in the visitors' room, reading a Houston paper. It was a long time before any prisoners were brought down from the cells, and the visitors, almost all Europeans, were standing around the table by one set of vending machines, talking. Two guys came over to speak to Maria and me. They were Scandinavians, Norwegian I think, and they knew we were there to visit Simon, and that this was his last day. I suppose everyone knew. They were very kind, speaking to us in heavily accented but very fluent English. They offered to drive us over to Chasserton, they said that they were planning to join the demonstration in the street, and that we might not be in a good state to drive back afterwards. Maria was uncertain. Americans nowadays have this thing about foreigners, but she took her lead from me. I had been worried about the idea of Maria doing all the driving. So it was agreed that they would wait outside the prison for us at noon, and that we would stop somewhere to eat on the way over. Then the men started to be brought down and the Norwegians (Hans and Ikval) went off to talk to the guy they were visiting.

When Simon was brought down the chaplain came over, and put his hand gently on Maria's shoulder. He asked if he could do anything, and gave us a map showing how to find the house in Chasserton where we were to meet him in the afternoon. He said that he would be with Simon on the journey over, that he would join us for a few minutes in the Drury Road house and then stay with Simon 'until after it was all over'. He and his colleague would talk with us after that. He checked on how we were to travel to Chasserton and seemed pleased with the Norwegians for being willing to take us over. He did warn us, however, that Maria mustn't leave the hire car in the prison car park. For one thing, we wouldn't be allowed back in to collect it, so he suggested we leave it at one of our hotels. He had a few words with Simon before we picked up the phones, and shook hands with us before he left.

Simon was subdued. He smiled bravely at Maria but she had tears in her eyes and I could see the muscles in Simon's face working as he tried to control himself.

"I'll give you a few minutes alone," I said, and sat at the table in

117

the middle of the room. The officer on duty crossed next to me to go to the drinks machine by the door, and gently touched my back as she passed. It seemed like an act of compassion but I couldn't look at her. Seeing Maria crying had brought tears to my own eyes and I was trying desperately to control myself. I tried to pray but it felt like mumbo-jumbo.

I joined them again about half an hour later. By then it was just after 10.30am and we only had until 12.00 noon. I was surprised, when I sat down and picked up my phone, to see that both Maria and Simon looked happy, or perhaps 'amused' is a better word. They weren't smiling bravely, with tears about to brim over, the way they had been when they greeted each other earlier, they were grinning. As soon as I had my ear to the phone Simon said, "We've been thinking about the funniest things." If a man can be said to giggle, Simon almost giggled.

"We were remembering the only vacation we ever took," explained Maria. "We were dirt poor and we thought we'd go camping. We borrowed this little tent … "

"Oh, and do you remember the bent pole?" interrupted Simon.

"Yes! Yes!" It was obviously hugely amusing to them. "We had no idea how to put it up…"

"Then that guy in the camper van told us there were bears around …"

"Ma was so scared she didn't sleep all night …"

"And we ate nothing but burgers for a week …"

"And pizza! Pizza too!"

Simon was doubled up with laughter. Guys from the regular cages were looking across at us, some looking worried, others grinning. I found myself laughing too, not at their stories but at their mirth and the sense of fun that surrounded them.

"We did have some good times, didn't we?" said Simon.

"Yea, we did, we really did," agreed Maria, and started to chuckle again.

After that the time passed lightly. It was like those moments at airports when the farewells are all done and you are just waiting to go through security when there will be nothing left but to wave at each other. I was vaguely aware of the Norwegians leaving before us, and then the chaplain came back and the officer and chaplain came over together and said, "Time's up."

We picked up our plastic wallets, I said, "God bless," and hung up my phone, giving Maria the last few seconds, and with shaky legs we walked out of the open door from the visitors' room.

The now familiar feeling of disconnection came over me again when we climbed into the Norwegians' beautiful SUV in the car park of Maria's motel. We stopped somewhere along the road for lunch, but neither Maria nor I ate anything. The Norwegians didn't try to talk to us, or we to them. The day had turned bright and the winter countryside looked lovely in the early afternoon sun, but everything felt strangely irrelevant. Maria said at one point, "This will have been the first time Pa has seen any countryside for more than a year," but none of us answered. He would be in Chasserton by now, in the cell next to the execution chamber. He was living a nightmare and we couldn't help him.

Later, as we approached the town and slowed down, Maria said, "He is innocent you know."

"Yes," I agreed.

"Ja," agreed a Norwegian. Again, nobody said anything further. What was there to say?

They gave us cups of coffee at the Drury Road house, sitting on soft, comfortable sofas in a lovely, spacious room with a pile of children's toys in one corner. While we were sipping our drinks the chaplain and his colleague arrived and the Norwegians left to join the protest. They talked us through the events which were to follow, and then Maria and I climbed into the car of the Drury Road host, and were driven to the prison.

I remember waiting in a room with painted breeze block walls and a water cooler in one corner, the only thing to make any noise. We were searched again and walked through another metal detector, and then we were told to wait. It was four thirty in the afternoon. For half an hour or so nobody came near us, but around five we

119

heard some noise in the corridor outside. "The victim's family," said Maria under her breath. "Not Simon's victim," I thought. "He didn't do it."

Some time after that the chaplain's colleague came in and told us that Simon was doing well. Texas discontinued last meals of the prisoner's choice a few years ago, and the new tradition is to give them chicken salad. Apparently he ate well, and had prayed with the chaplains, and was, we were told, 'ready'. Really? Could anyone be ready?

We were escorted across a sort of footbridge to another building, and along a footpath past some well-laid lawn. We could hear the street protest. We were joined by men in suits and open necked shirts – journalists and officials of some sort, and led to an office, where again we had to wait. Maria held my hand and the journalists stood by a door talking quietly, then one gave a shout of laughter. This was just work for them. Then we were escorted to the viewing room.

Simon was already on the gurney, his right arm strapped to a sort of wing, with an IV tube already in his vein. He had a white blanket over him, with straps tightly over that. He smiled at us as we came in, a slightly quavery smile.

We were offered the front row, so to speak. I mean we were up close to the glass. There was a wall next to Maria, and from beyond it we could hear talking – the victim's family, there to see that justice was done. Simon was asked if he wanted to say anything. There was a microphone hanging from the ceiling, and we could see Simon looking at us. I expected him to say something, I don't know, special. I thought that these would be his very last words on this earth, and whatever they were, I would never forget them. I thought that these words would live in Maria's heart for the rest of her life. I thought he might claim his innocence again, for the last time, and that he would tell Maria he loved her, and I wanted to hear him say those things, and I wanted everyone to hear them.

Then he started talking. We could see his mouth moving, the muscles on his face changing as he expressed different thoughts, but somehow we couldn't hear any thing. For a few seconds I just stood there, we all did. I thought someone would do something, press a button or something, but nobody moved. Simon was still talking, he was smiling, then he must have seen the expression on Maria's face. He frowned, and seemed to say something to someone out of sight, at the foot of the gurney. Had he realised we couldn't hear him? He tried to raise himself but he was tightly strapped down. Maria looked around, behind us, and then into the death chamber.

"I can't hear!" she screamed, but still nobody did anything. "I want to hear my pa!"

Simon tried to move again, but he was too firmly strapped down. He could see that Maria was terribly upset. Of course he didn't know what was happening. He turned away from the window and seemed to address another comment to the person we couldn't see. It felt like being stuck in a nightmare, when you run and run but get nowhere. I looked behind me but the journalists and officials looked calm, even disinterested. Maria started to hammer on the glass with her fists and an official came forward and pulled her back, away from the window. Simon could see that something was badly wrong. He strained against the straps that held him to the gurney, twisting towards Maria, then looking away again to the person we couldn't see.

"Please …" I started to say, then Maria screamed again.

"No!" she shouted, "No! No! No!"

Her father had closed his eyes. His body gave a light jerk, the sort of movement you sometimes see in someone as they fall into a deep sleep. His face was still turned slightly away from us but I could see the muscles around his eyes seem to twitch, then relax.

Then the microphone was working again. A disembodied voice: the warden? A doctor? – standing at the foot of the gurney out of sight for us, said, "I pronounce Simon Leroy McKellar dead. 6.11pm."

At the Drury Road house afterwards they apologised for the microphone breaking down. They said that Simon had made a death bed confession, withdrawing his claims of innocence and apologising to the victim's family. They promised to send us a full transcript of his last words. They said he had 'died well'. I don't believe for one minute that was what he said. Not for one second.

Sunday 16th January 8.00am

I am feeling pretty confused, I have been ever since the last diary entry. So much has happened in the three days since that it is hard to take it all in. Well, I have all day, and I plan to sit here and think about it all, holding it in the Light and letting order be restored, if possible, into my life.

After the last diary entry I spent a long time sitting in my room, reliving the events I had recorded. In fact, it seemed almost impossible to do anything else. The experience had been so intense that it seemed I couldn't digest it, and my mind wanted to run over it again and again. I needed to pack, because I was checking out when Maria picked me up at 11.00am although I intended to keep my bags behind the counter at Reception. My taxi wasn't collecting me until close to 5.00pm. I found it really difficult to organise myself, though. For example, when I travel I always carry a plastic laundry bag from a hotel, into which I put my dirty clothes. On Wednesday evening I had just tossed the blouse I had worn all day into the corner, not put it properly in the bag, but when I picked it up on Thursday morning something about the butterfly pattern on the sleeves suddenly took me back to that observation room, and me looking at my arm as Maria and I held hands, and I was there again, just as I had been when I heard the television announcement at breakfast time. It is hard to explain. I knew I was in my hotel room holding a dirty blouse, but I felt as if I were facing the death chamber and, as if I were in a nightmare, I felt I needed to do something to stop Simon from being murdered, but I was frozen and at the same time my heart was pounding. I don't know how long I stayed like that, but gradually I seemed to move back into the present, and I found myself still holding the blouse in a sweaty hand, sitting on the floor and trembling all over.

I put the television on, choosing the weather channel, but then discovered that even they broadcast the news every half hour. I was just sorting out the stuff I put on my bedside table, when I heard Simon's execution and deathbed confession reported all over again, and again my heart started to pound and my legs felt shaky.

I managed to pack, then I went back to the lobby and ate a bowl of some sweet, orange-coloured cereal, and checked out in time for Maria to pick me up.

We were both in quite a state, of course. We didn't say much over coffee at some place on the edge of Stanley, but Maria wept for a while as we drove to Chasserton. She had to sign some forms in the administrative area of the prison. Simon's body is to be cremated and the ashes sent back to Corpus Christi for scattering. The chaplain saw us (I was waiting in a sort of entrance lobby, because I am not family, Maria was standing at a counter a few yards away) and greeted us as if we were just casual acquaintances, then went away and came back with sealed envelopes for us both. "Simon's last words," he said. "We're really sorry about the microphone yesterday. It shouldn't have happened …" then he saw someone through an office door and called out, "Officer Johnson!" and was gone, on more important business, no doubt.

Afterwards we went to a pancake house in Chasserton and, to be honest, we both ate quite a lot. Neither of us had eaten much the day before and now that the forms were signed, the business part of the day was over. Maria was going to stay one more night, and then drive down to Houston to fly home on Friday afternoon, and I was booked into the airport hotel for Thursday night, to fly back to London overnight on Friday. After we had eaten we opened our envelopes and read the words which we were supposed to believe were Simon's last words. They didn't sound like him at all, as I had expected. They said nothing about him loving Maria, either, I am absolutely convinced he would have said that. Maria cried again to the obvious concern of our overweight pancake waitress, but I just felt angry. We were back at my hotel not long after 4.00pm and the taxi arrived before five.

I didn't realise I had lost this journal until after breakfast on Friday. I had actually slept for about five hours, and although I woke in the middle of a nightmare, once I was fully awake I felt okay. I went downstairs and had the hot buffet with lots of coffee, and came back up to my room intending to do some serious meditation or praying.

At first when I couldn't find my journal I thought I had just packed badly. I was in quite a state on Thursday morning. I upturned everything on the bed, but still I couldn't find it. I tried to think when I had last seen it, and realised that when I sat in the Stanley hotel I tended to use the window sill as a table. I must have left my journal there. I found myself going hot and cold. What had I written in that journal that I would rather nobody over here read? The big thing was my belief in Simon's innocence, and I tried to remember what I had written about the supposed confession.

Then logic took over. If a room maid found my journal, would she read it? Probably not. Those cleaners are expected to do a huge amount in a very small period of time. Probably she would either throw it away or hand it in to Reception.

I phoned the Stanley hotel but they said they hadn't found it. I searched through my stuff again but it wasn't there, and I was stumped – I really didn't know what to do. I sat in silence and I read some of the Gideon Bible, but it was really hard to focus. I tried using writing paper from the bureau in the room to note down my thoughts, but it didn't feel right, and anyhow I was very uneasy. I checked my emails. There were lots of kind messages from home, and an email from Maria wishing me a good journey. Then I watched a film on television until I needed to check out. I looked under the bed and in all the drawers in the room before I left, hoping I had somehow unpacked my journal in a daze and forgotten where I'd put it, but it was nowhere to be seen. It was annoying as well as worrying, because I wasn't sure I would ever have the courage to record Simon's execution all over again. It was hard enough doing it once.

Everything seemed normal when I got to the airport. They like passengers to check in online or via the machines but last time I visited the States, and again on my way out this time, it didn't work for me and I had to do it at the desk. I wasn't worried when that happened again. I swiped my passport and the message came up, 'Report to Desk' and, knowing the routine, I wheeled my way over and waited in line while a man in a very smart white tracksuit checked in an equally smart white golf bag. Then it was my turn.

I handed over my passport and my DeV with the e-ticket code displayed and expected, as usual, for the officer behind the desk to tap a few keys on his computer and to give me my boarding card. Instead he said, "Wait here a minute, Ma'am," and took my passport behind a sort of rubber curtain that served as a door.

I waited, still not feeling in the least bit concerned. Someone came over and opened the next door check-in desk, then started dealing with the people in the small queue behind me. The people shuffled to the right. I continued to wait.

After about ten minutes the officer came back, still holding my passport, and lifted the counter next to his desk, switching off the lights at the same time so that his area was closed. "Will you come this way, please?" he said, perfectly politely.

I wheeled my bag through the gap, he held the rubber curtain aside, and we walked down a short, narrow corridor into a small windowless office.

"Please take a seat," he offered. "Someone will be with you in a minute." He closed the door as he left.

I used not to be suspicious, in my youth, but contact with Karl and the events of the last five or so months have made me less trusting. I could not see a camera in the room but that did not mean there was not one there. I wondered how I should behave. Was it better to look a little nervous, as any law-abiding person would, who was unused to being led aside into windowless rooms like this? Or was it better to look totally relaxed, knowing I was innocent of any wrongdoing? Then it occurred to me that perhaps I should ignore any possible surveillance and follow my instincts. So I settled myself more comfortably on the plastic chair, held my hands open and cupped on my lap as I do in worship, closed my eyes and tried to think of the True Light, which gives light to every person. For a short while I was still aware of possible cameras, and if I had let myself I could have started wondering what somebody observing me might think, but quite quickly my mind focussed on the golden glow I sometimes picture, and then a quiet peace started to settle on me. It was just like being in a Meeting for Worship. I felt comforted, even settled, and slowly a conviction seemed to drift over me that somehow everything would be all right. I did not *hear* a voice, but perhaps I *felt* a voice, except that makes no sense. There was no clock in the room and I hadn't looked at my watch, but I stayed like that long enough for a deep calm to settle inside me. When the door opened again I felt totally untroubled.

"There seems to be a problem with your passport," said a large woman as she entered. "We need to ask you a few questions. Will you come this way?"

I went to pick up my shoulder bag, but she put her hand out to stop me. "Please leave all your luggage here, Ma'am," she commanded. "We'll need to search it. It'll be returned to you later," and she led me out of the room.

Deputy Williamson had a large desk and several filing cabinets, as well as a DeV with a huge free standing screen in her office, but still no window, I noticed. She opened my passport and scrutinized it, then started tapping on her keyboard. After several minutes in which nobody said anything she asked, abruptly, "Reason for visit?"

Obviously they would already know that. "I came to be with my friend Simon and to witness his execution," I said.

She didn't comment, but tapped more keys. Then, "Date of arrival?"

"8th January," I replied. "Last Saturday."

Another silence followed. More key tapping, quite a lot more than it would take to enter 'Saturday 8th January' onto a form.

Deputy Williamson sighed. "Port of embarkation?"

"I flew from Heathrow."

"With whom have you been in contact here in the United States?"

I thought carefully. "Well, just Simon McKellar and his daughter Maria," I said.

She looked up sharply, staring at me with a frown. "That is not our information," she stated coldly. "Please tell me all the people you have been in contact with since your arrival."

What did she want? I thought back through my visit. "I stayed at the Garden Suburb Airport Hotel," I said, "so I will have spoken to a receptionist there when I checked in, and another when I checked out, and to some waitresses. I took the hotel car from the airport and I will have spoken to the driver ..."

She looked angry. "Don't mess with me!" she warned.

I stayed silent. So did she.

"How did you get to Stanley?" she finally barked.

"I took a taxi."

"Taxi company? Driver's name?"

"I don't remember. I still have the card in my shoulder bag but it's in the other room ..."

She made a sort of grump under her breath and typed some more.

Then, "Who did you meet in Stanley?"

"I checked in, so I spoke to the receptionist there, actually it was the manageress. I spoke to the woman who tidies the breakfast area. I had one taxi ride to the prison, and I ate at the Tex-Mex on my own once. With Maria McKellar ..."

"All this is nonsense!" exclaimed Deputy Williamson. "I want to know who you met. Who did you arrange to see? Who are your contacts in Stanley?"

I looked at her. Her face was red and she was frowning. She had her legs crossed under the desk and she was jiggling one leg impatiently. I wondered what she wanted to know, and what she thought was going on. I have no contacts in Stanley and there was nothing I could tell her. I still felt very calm.

She tried again. "Our information suggests that you drove to Indian Village and met a contact there on Monday 19th January at 2.00pm. Why have you not told me about this?"

"That's crazy," I said. "At 2.00pm I was in the prison visiting Simon McKellar. I handed my passport in when I went through security and the officer logged the time. I left the prison around 5.00pm and the officer logged the time when she returned my passport. I didn't hire a car. I've already told you I used taxis until I met up with Maria McKellar."

Deputy Williamson glared at me. I didn't glare back. I felt very calm, and even slightly sorry for her, because obviously she wanted something from me which she wasn't going to get. Someone had given her some wrong information. She looked away from me, glancing up at the wall behind me as if she were checking something, so that I felt like turning round to see what was there, then she looked back at her DeV and typed some more.

After a couple of minutes she stopped. "Come this way, please," she commanded and led me back down the narrow white corridor into the room where I had waited before. My shoulder bag with my DeV in it and my suitcase had gone. "Wait here," she demanded and closed the door behind her.

Without my shoulder bag I felt a bit lost. It wasn't just that my DeV was in there, all the other things you need when you're travelling were in that bag: tissues, a couple of painkillers, my credit and debit cards, a comb … and where was my passport now? I started to feel a sort of panic rising inside me. I had no way of contacting anyone. Nobody knew where I was. More than an hour had passed and if they didn't let me go soon I would miss my plane. Karl was supposed to be meeting me … I got up and tried the door, but of course it wouldn't open. I thought I would try to be calm again, and worship, but my heart was beating hard and I could feel sweat on my forehead, and I couldn't concentrate. There was nothing on the walls of the room to look at, they were just plain white with pale grey skirting. I looked down at my jeans, which are quite old but which I feel good in, and I remembered buying them more than a year earlier. Somehow, oddly, that helped. I decided to trace my journey from the flat to the store in the middle of town, by the pizza place. How many post boxes were there on that route?

How many roads did I have to cross? And somehow, concentrating on those things calmed me almost as much as worship did.

When the door next opened it was a male officer. He walked in and held out his hand, as if to shake mine, as if he were one of Amy's friends and we were being introduced before G and Ts. "I'm real sorry to have made you wait," he said in a deep, southern voice. "We seem to have some problems here. We'll have to ask you to stay while we sort it all out."

"Here!" I exclaimed. How long was I going to have to sit on that plastic chair in that empty room?

He smiled, just a courtesy smile, nothing more. "Here in Houston," he said. "I'll get one of my men to drive you back to your hotel."

"I don't have a reservation!" I said. "Where's my luggage? I don't even have my credit cards! I'd like to see the British consul."

The officer sighed. "Ma'am, you don't need a consul now, because of the Special Relationship, remember? We'll arrange a room for you and you can buy what you need at the hotel shop. You can pay us back when all this is sorted out ."

"But…"

He wasn't listening. He held the door open for me, we walked further down the white corridor and out through a door to one of those semi-derelict areas you often see around airports, and there was a police car and a driver, and back I went to the hotel.

The last two days have been very strange. I have a pleasant room, similar to the one I checked out of, but looking the other way, so that I can see more green. Following the instructions of the policeman who drove me, I went into the hotel shop, 'bought' several T-shirts (they all say things like 'Houston Texans Rule the World' or 'H – T – NFL champs') to wear at night or while I'm laundering the clothes I was standing up in, a toothbrush, a comb and a pen. Of course when I bought this stuff I didn't know how long I'd be here, and I wanted some clean underwear, but those shops aren't designed for people doing a full clothes shop. The only underwear they sold was gimmicky, the sort of thing a man might buy for a girlfriend on the way home from a business trip. I bought two thongs, pink with pictures of a Native North American Chief in full headdress on the only sizeable patch of material, and a pair of stars and stripes socks, and made do with the soap, shampoo and so on in the room. I have a room card with some special marking on it which I am able to use as a sort of swipe card. It's the same with meals. Of course, until about an hour ago it meant that if I left the hotel I had no currency at all.

I wish I were the sort of person who remembers phone numbers, but all the numbers I use are on my DeV or in an old-fashioned little address book in a drawer in my kitchen, so I couldn't phone anyone back home. I felt glad that Karl was supposed to be meeting me at Heathrow, he would know what to do when I wasn't on that flight, better than anyone else I know. I spent my time watching mindless TV and exploring the hotel from top to bottom. I've drunk a lot of coffee at the concession in the main hotel concourse, because it's slightly more interesting sitting there watching people come and go than sitting up here, but I hate to think what sort of bill I will have accumulated, which I'll now have to settle.

I was sitting in a big, brown leather chair next to an amazing (but artificial) display of lilies and greenery, opposite the reception desk, when my suitcase and shoulder bag arrived. I saw the police car pull up where the airport taxis stop, and I watched as the officer wheeled my case into the building. He was also carrying a large blue plastic bag with black printing on it. He went over to the desk and said something to the woman at reception, and she nodded her head towards me. The officer turned and came over.

"I have your baggage, Ma'am," he said. He put the case next to my chair and passed me the plastic bag. It was my shoulder bag, sealed up and labelled 'Homeland Security'. "And I have been asked to tell you that you are to report to Desk 7, Terminal D for your flight to Heathrow, which leaves at 18.20." He handed me a paper wallet. I opened it. There was my passport and a boarding card, the latter also stamped 'Homeland Security'.

I had stood when he started to talk to me, and I remained

standing. I was clutching the big blue Homeland Security plastic bag, and I had the documents in my hand too. I wish I had thought of something sensible to say, but I was completely taken aback. Surely he would give me some sort of an explanation? Apologise for their mistake? The officer just looked at me, added "Thank you for your cooperation, Ma'am," touched his cap and turned, and left.

Back in this room, I first extricated my shoulder bag with some difficulty from the well sealed blue plastic, and checked its contents. As far as I can tell everything important is here. If there is anything missing it will be some of those cards I accumulate everywhere I go: loyalty cards, restaurant cards, cards with change-of-email-address information, and I'll only realise they are missing if I ever want them again. Both credit cards and my debit card are here. There's still $50 and some change in my purse. My DeV is here, and seems to be fully charged. The little notebook where I write shopping lists was in the inside pocket where I always keep it, but the flimsy cover is torn and smudged. I wonder what interest Homeland Security could have in items such as 'Post Office, stamps/white envelopes/b-card for M' or 'Tomatoes, ice-cream, salmon fillets'. My pens are all in my pencil case but the emery board has gone, and my little packet of tissues is missing too. My cross and chain, which I keep in my purse when I'm not wearing it, was in with my rail card. Obviously they have checked everything.

Then I opened my case. It was very neatly packed, much more neatly than I had left it. Each item was carefully folded, and small things were tucked down the side. It felt odd, thinking that someone had looked through all my clothes, my wash bag, even my make-up bag, had taken my dirty laundry out of the laundry bag and looked through it, before folding it and re-packing as if it were all fresh and clean. I took everything out, item by item, and there, halfway down, between my pyjama top and my blue striped t-shirt, was this journal.

I have to check out by 2.00pm if I don't want to pay extra. That gives me nearly an hour. I plan to phone Karl and email as many people as I can in that time, and then get the hotel car to the airport. I'll eat lunch there, and hope that the check in works this time. I feel sure it will.

CHAPTER 4

I am sitting up in bed, the sofa bed in Karl's flat, and I cannot sleep. My thoughts are going round and round in my head, I am jet lagged, I still feel stunned about Simon's death, and so much has happened since… I have tried to calm myself by sitting in the Light, but all that happens is that I listen to the blood pounding in my ears, and then I find myself reliving the feeling of being in that small white room at the airport, or finding my journal underneath my pyjama top, or watching Simon trying to talk to us and no sound reaching us … I feel a sort of panic welling up inside me, and I want everything just to stop, to let me catch up.

It doesn't look as if everything is going to stop, though. After my last journal entry I opened my DeV and after a bit of difficulty (I had to go through a lot of security questions with my server) I finally opened the computer element. There were loads of emails. I usually check them once or twice a day and of course I hadn't read them since the day after Simon's execution. I started at the top, with the most recent ones. I deleted without even glancing at the travel offers, the free vouchers, the Amnesty requests for urgent action and the charity appeals. There was some ordinary community business from Meeting, which I reckoned I would deal with when I got home. Then there was an email from Fran posted on Sunday at 7.52 local time, the time Fran got up to go to Meeting, an odd time to send emails. It was short and to the point, with no frills and no personal comments. It just said, 'Sabina and Imran deported yesterday. Not sure about Yasmin. Activities not conducive to the

133

common good.' I stared and stared at it. Deported? But they are as English as me! Deported to where? I scrolled down the other emails, but there was nothing from Sabina. What could have happened?

I went back to the top of the page and ignored the next couple of postings, an e-card from Amy welcoming me home, asking if I had coped all right and wondering whether I'd like to have dinner with her on Wednesday after a swim, so she obviously didn't know I'd been stuck in Houston, and a request for financial aid for orphans in the Caribbean. I nearly skipped the email and attachment from Pru, the clerk of Meeting, but the title of the posting, 'Park Encampment Harbours Terrorists' made me open it. There was a newspaper account attached to a note from Pru, 'Thought you might be interested.' It was from a national paper, not from the *Messenger*, and it was very brief: 'An ATTF spokesman confirmed yesterday, in response to a freedom of information request from this paper, that known terrorists have been observed in a number of tent encampments around the country, including one in a city centre recreation park in the south of England and two in central London. Appropriate measures have been taken.' There was an email sent at 20.07 on Saturday, also from Fran, 'Where are you?' it said.

A bit further down were emails which had been sent during the day on Saturday. There was another from Fran, 'Tried phoning. I suppose you are still asleep. Do you want to come over this evening and tell us all about it?' Then there was one from Jo sent just after lunch, 'Lots happening. Claire and Jamie staying with us. They send their love. See you soon.' Sent earlier still were a number of messages from friends commiserating with me on Simon's execution, and expressing the usual kind thoughts and reflections one hears following a death. They were kind emails from generous hearted people, but with all that has happened since the beginning of Wednesday they seemed bland.

There was nothing at all from Karl. I checked through three times, and scanned my spam, but there was nothing. I even went through the trash folder in case I had deleted something by accident. Nothing. Then I looked at my watch, realised I needed to check out and settle my huge bill, and that I hadn't actually answered anyone. Well, it was too late now.

In the lift going down all I could think was, "Sabina and Imran have been deported? Where are they now?"

Checking in and going through security was totally straightforward. Desk 7, where I had been told to report, was just one of five open desks, and the 'Homeland Security' stamp on my boarding card seemed not to cause any interest at any point. I found a place near my departure gate that served salads, and it was just as I finished eating that the text came through from Karl: 'See you at arrivals, 6.45am'. Somehow that text brought me more comfort than all the emails expressing sympathy, that I had read in the hotel.

There is something deeply uncomfortable about arriving after an overnight flight. I felt dirty, and my jeans felt baggy at the knees and the seat from sitting for too long. I needed to clean my teeth, I felt as if my hair needed washing, and my stomach was uncomfortable. They never give you enough coffee at breakfast on planes.

But it was so good to see Karl! He was standing to one side among taxi drivers, American forces personnel and holiday tour representatives, looking friendly and somehow clean. He was wearing a thick petrol blue jacket with the collar up, and proper trousers, not jeans, with tan boots that looked like walking boots. He smiled as soon as he saw me, and kissed my cheek before he took my case.

"The car's this way," he said, leading towards the short stay car park. Then, over his shoulder, he said, "Bit of a rough trip, then?"

An odd thing happened in the multi-storey. Instead of walking straight to the car, when we got out of the lift on floor E Karl walked over to the edge, where you can see over the barrier wall and across to some other buildings ('Ameri-freight' proclaimed the nearest building, in cream letters), or down to some sort of access road below. It was not quite eight in the morning, still greyish-dark in the English drizzle, and rather depressing. Leaning out as if looking for something, Karl said, "Don't talk in the car, about anything important. Okay?" Then we headed across the concrete to the place where he had parked.

We didn't speak until Karl had driven out past the ticket machine (he didn't pay, the barrier came up as we approached. Something to do with the ATTF barcode on the car I think). As we followed the endless road which seems to go round and round Heathrow before you finally start actually going somewhere, Karl said, "You missed some horrible weather over here. There's been flooding in the Midlands again. Did you hear?" And following his lead we discussed the relative climates of Texas and England, then the books we had been reading, and the New Year's Eve party at Amy's, which was the last time we'd met. Only in an anonymous service station, drinking coffee in a half empty restaurant with dirty cups and plates littering the surrounding tables and a floor slippery from the moisture walked in by travellers, did Karl say anything significant. "Things aren't very straightforward," he said. "I'm sure you realise by now. We'll go back to your flat, and see how the land lies, then take it from there. Okay?"

"Yes, but …" I didn't really know what he meant. I was longing to settle down with Fran and Jo to discuss everything that had happened in the last week. I was longing to sit at my French windows looking out on the winter garden and across the park, with my feet on the warm flooring, and just be my normal self again. Adventures in books sound fun, and if you listen on the radio to people who have had travel dramas it can seem as if you've lived a very ordinary life, but I was tired, fed up and confused. Karl was stirring the froth in his empty coffee cup with a teaspoon (it was lovely to see metal teaspoons, even after only a week of plastic spoons and wooden stirrers in Texas) but he put the spoon down and briefly touched my hand. "I know," he said, "I know." Then, more briskly, "Come on then, let's get you home."

It seemed I was not to fulfil my wish of sleeping in my own bed, talking to my friends or sitting at my own window. As soon as I put the key in the lock of my front door I knew something was wrong. It didn't turn properly, and then it moved suddenly, as if it had been stuck, and when I walked in somehow the flat felt different. It was almost a smell, almost a feeling in the air. Karl came in behind me, glanced at my face and said in a jovial way, not quite like his usual voice, "Welcome home! Let me make some coffee."

As I took my case through to the bedroom, he went into the kitchen. Almost at once he came back with the pad I keep on the fridge, on which he had written, 'Has someone been here?' I was looking at my bedside table which didn't look quite right. Everything was there that should have been, the old photo of my parents, the picture of Amy's family, a box of tissues, but somehow … I never put the tissues on the edge like that, I tend to knock them onto the floor at night, and I usually put tissues in a blue box in my room, to match the décor. I had a thought. I went through to the spare room, and found the blue box there, where the pink box should have been. And the teddy bear, the door stop, was on the bed. Had I put it there before I left? It wasn't impossible but I didn't think so … I looked at Karl who had followed me through, and shook my head negatively.

"We forgot to pick up any milk," said Karl, "I'll go and get some."

"I'll come with you," I said. "I need to keep moving or I'll go to sleep."

Karl grinned at me approvingly, but then said in a very unsmiling voice. "Okay, if we're going to the supermarket I could do with getting some food for tonight. Will you mind?"

"No, that's fine," I agreed, and went through to the living room to pick up my shoulder bag. To my surprise Karl picked up my case again, but I didn't say anything, and we went back down to his car.

So now here I am. We washed my clothes at Karl's place, and repacked my case with a thick fleecy jumper of Karl's and a couple of pairs of snugly blue socks as well as my Texas stuff, and after I had noted in the back of this journal all the phone numbers I might need, Karl took my DeV and got rid of it somewhere. We discussed what to do about my internet access as we walked round the supermarket, it really isn't possible to manage without some sort of DeV now days, and in the end Karl bought me a rather sweet little DeV 14. He thinks I can be traced from my old one. He checked his car thoroughly. He thought someone might have got to it while he was waiting at arrivals, but it seemed clear of bugs, and Karl obviously doesn't believe that they would put surveillance into his flat. Today we will drive to Wales, to a place he knows, until he can sort out what is going on.

He saw this journal in my case while I was repacking. "I hope you haven't put anything that could be … misunderstood … in there," he said. "Although I suppose anything can be misunderstood if a person puts his mind to it…"

Wednesday 19th January 10.40am

Under different circumstances the place where I find myself now could seem magical. I am sitting in one of three mismatched armchairs, looking out of a low window set into a stone wall that must be more than a foot deep. The floor of this little room is made of old-fashioned quarry tiles with damp marks on them, and there is a strange green rug spread across the centre of the room. I have a steaming cup of coffee on the wide windowsill in front of me, next to a vase of holly which Karl and I cut this morning after breakfast, from a variegated bush by the back door. Beyond the holly, beyond the glass of the window, is a narrow lane and a fence, and beyond the fence is a rough meadow with sheep in it. Beyond the meadow, with a streak of green-gold light where the sun is breaking through some rolling clouds, are hills, not quite high enough to be called mountains, but big enough to put anything in the south of England to shame. Behind me, as I sit here, is a door through to a little kitchen, which we stocked with bags full of food yesterday. There is a little bathroom, rather damp and cold, at the back of the cottage, and a door to some steep wooden steps, almost a ladder, leading to the one bedroom upstairs. Nothing in the cottage matches anything else. It seems to have been furnished from other people's cast-offs. The windows are small and single-glazed, I see now why Karl put his snugly jumper into my case, and there are candles everywhere as if the power might fail at any time. Nevertheless there is a lovely feel to this place, a sort of calm, which might be to do with how remote it is, but which feels like a characteristic of the cottage itself. There is some strange sort of old fashioned electrical heating so that although there are draughts by the windows, the room is warm, and all I can hear is sheep. Earlier there were birds sweeping low across the meadow, but I can hear no birdsong now. Somewhere at the back of the cottage there is the steady drip, drip of some guttering after an earlier rain storm, and I think it might rain again.

I have given up trying to make sense of all this. It was a long drive yesterday, first on busy main roads but for the last twenty or more miles on smaller and smaller lanes, until finally, at around four, in the cold, wet dusk of a Welsh afternoon, we arrived. Karl had a key to the back door, and let us into a bitterly cold, drab-looking room, and my heart sank. But we dumped our bags, Karl flicked a few switches, heating units started to click as they warmed up, and by the time we had driven a further fifteen miles or more to a supermarket and back (our second supermarket visit in less than two days, although this time Karl paid in cash), the cottage was warm and welcoming.

So here I am. Karl cooked a lovely meal last night, pork with all sorts of vegetables in a cheese sauce, and pasta, and we ate orange mousse afterwards. We bought several bottles of wine and opened one to go with our dinner. The cotton curtains were closed and we brought down one of the lamps from upstairs to create a softer glow than the overhead light offered. For the first time in ages I felt really secure.

As Karl poured the last of the wine into our glasses I said, "What's going on, Karl?"

"I don't know." He stared at a picture of a ram, hanging on the wall opposite, and sighed.

"Is it to do with the tent school? Or is it something else? When they kept me in Houston … I can't see why they should be worried one way or the other over there, about what we do here …"

"Well," Karl rubbed his eyes, as if he were suddenly very tired. "It's probably not the school, exactly. It's your underlying attitude:

you, Fran, Jo, your whole community really, although all the time someone doesn't *do* anything, nobody really cares what they believe. Your mistake has been doing something."

"But …" It seemed ridiculous. All this for three part-time classes in a makeshift school in a temporary tent city? "Karl, it's just a school! And they've deported Sabina and Imran!"

"Yes." He continued to stare at the picture.

"But it wasn't our security people who stopped me travelling," I reminded him.

"No."

Another silence.

Then Karl said, "I read that Simon confessed before he died."

"No!" I was really angry. "No, he didn't!" And I told Karl what had happened.

Karl finished his wine. Then he looked directly at me. "How did you get to be this old and still be so naïve ?" he wondered. Then he asked, "So you think the authorities over there lied?"

"Of course they did! It was obviously rigged. The sound came back as soon as the Warden wanted to announce he was dead!"

"Quite," Karl said. "So you resist the actions of our government, our freely elected, democratic government over here, by starting that school, and then you go there and you witness something worse, a bigger injustice. Do you blame them for being suspicious about what else you might do?"

I gulped, and coughed over the last of my wine. "But…"

"Look at it from their point of view," Karl suggested. "They believe in what they're doing. Okay, there's some corruption, but to many of them there probably doesn't seem to be any alternative. Politics is a messy business, you know." He sighed. "In a way you lot take the easy option."

"What easy option?" I really couldn't see what he meant.

"You stand outside and look in," Karl explained.

Now Karl has left. He went after breakfast, leaving me with, he said, everything I might need for a week or so while he sorts things out. I'm not sure what he is going to sort out, or why. I feel safe here,

140

but I also feel worried. I haven't made contact with anyone since I got back. There are unanswered emails from Jo and Fran and from Amy, and from the clerk of Meeting. There are things I don't understand. Why are Claire and Jamie at Jo's?

Now that I think about it, nothing that has happened to me in the last week or more makes any sense. Simon's 'confession' was obviously rigged but to be honest that is really not significant given the blatant injustices of the death penalty, 'experts' giving false evidence, jailhouse snitches claiming people have confessed and getting off almost scot-free themselves, corrupt attorneys, judges who boast about the number they have sentenced to death ... Simon's wasn't even a high profile case. And why deport Sabina and Imran? If they didn't like what we were doing, surely they had enough power just to close the school, or even to bulldoze the tent city?

I am perplexed, too, that Karl has said that we take the easy option. There are groups of people, mostly religious groups as far as I know, who choose to stay right out of politics, but our group is not like that. Right from the start we have always engaged in the world in which we live.

But even as I read back over what I have written I realise that maybe this is the problem. Perhaps it would be easier for those in authority if we were quieter, if we minded our own business. I suppose we mind *their* business, and that is what they don't like. I think Karl is wrong, I don't think we have chosen the easier option, but I do think we have chosen the more straightforward path. The way we approach things, we don't have to compromise. In our way of speaking, we can 'live in the Light'. I think Karl is a good man, but I'm quite sure his life is full of compromises and deviousness, or untruths, half truths and silences. He thinks I am naïve, but I don't really think that is right. I am, perhaps, idealistic, but I'm not even sure about that. I think that it is just that I seek Truth, not power or even other 'good' ends like an orderly society or economic growth.

Goodness, that sounds so pompous! Since it seems I will be here for about a week I think I will try to use this time to calm myself after such a strange few days, and also to recover from my jet lag, and generally to settle myself and get my life back into proportion. I have my new DeV with me, but I agreed with Karl not to access my emails or do anything to show 'them' where I am, or who is using this device. There is no TV in the cottage but of course I can get radio and television with the equipment I have. I'll try to introduce a bit of routine into my life. When I've written this journal entry the first thing I want to do is to explore the house and its surroundings, and then catch up with the news. I might do some housework too. I think this cottage is perhaps used as a holiday home. It is not as clean as I would like, but I can remedy that easily enough. And there are lots of books on shelves in the one upstairs room, so I'll see what is of interest there. It will be a challenge not being able to download any novels but of course I can't use any of my online accounts. Well, people used to manage fifty years ago, and I'm sure I can now.

But first I think I'll pause and just let the peace that is surrounding me, the gentle noises of the countryside and the warmth of this odd little cosy room, seep into my spirit, to cleanse me and to begin to iron out the bumps and wrinkles of all that has happened.

Thursday 20th January 8.00am

Karl has brought me to a lovely place. Yesterday worked out really well. It was so good to be on my own, in control of what I was doing. I sat for more than an hour after writing my last journal entry, sometimes with my eyes open, watching the sheep in the field opposite, and sometimes with my eyes closed, concentrating on what I could hear and on my own slow breathing. I remember an occasion from when I was a child. I had woken up frightened about something, a dream perhaps or a loud noise in the house, I was always a light sleeper. I suppose I had cried or called out, and my mother came in to comfort me. I can remember quite clearly her kneeling by the bed, stroking my hair. I lay there with my eyes closed and felt her hand, gentle on my head. Each time she stopped, thinking I had gone back to sleep, I opened my eyes and pleaded with her not to go away. I can't remember the end of the incident. Perhaps eventually I dozed off again, or maybe she told me that this was enough, I was to turn over and go back to sleep. Sitting by the window yesterday was the same feeling as that almost-forgotten occasion in my childhood. I felt as if I were being gently, calmly stroked. When finally I stood up, I felt physically strong, and optimistic.

First I explored the cottage. It didn't take long, but it was productive. Among the books upstairs I found some musty editions of religious tomes no doubt long out of print, including several that look quite interesting, if a little quaint. There is a part set of Dickens, which could keep me going for ages. I think I have read virtually all of Dickens except *Pickwick Papers* and some of the Christmas stories, but they bear reading more than once, and although I know the stories of the famous ones like *Oliver Twist* or *Great Expectations* I am not really familiar with the original texts, and will enjoy discovering them. I also found several books about birds and one about flowers. I will miss the books I had on my DeV: our own book of discipline and a copy of the Bible, and I can't download these things without giving my password and credit card number, and there seems to be no Bible in the cottage. Still, we are not among 'the People of the Book' as Muhammad (pbuh) called Christians and Jews, we are 'The People of the Spirit'. If I can sit in silence that is really all that I need.

Another great find was in a trunk next to the old-fashioned electric fire in this downstairs room. The fire is black and looks like a wood-burning stove, the sort of thing Amy has in her breakfast room. However, it is actually runs from the mains on a timer, and switches itself on (thanks to Karl, who set it before he left) at 7.00 every morning. Beside it is this black tin trunk, dented and (until yesterday afternoon) decidedly dusty, but inside were lots of useful things: a first aid kit in a green zip-up case, a sewing kit in a cardboard box, an old biscuit tin containing paper clips, rubber bands, an emery board, two safety pins and a box of matches with the name of a French hotel printed on the box, and a plastic bag full of oddments of wool. At first I thought I wasn't going to find any knitting needles, which would have been tantalizing, but I reasoned that if someone brought wool here they would surely bring needles too, so I searched around and found a plastic box of knitting needles behind the mugs in the sideboard! Also in the trunk was a very old road map, and with it I was able to locate more or less where I am, somewhere in the middle of Wales. It was hard to tell without the sat nav, and I'm not totally sure now that I have my exact location, but I must be pretty close.

By then it was lunch time. I organised biscuits and cheese and settled down with another coffee and one of the religious books (a biography of an American pioneer), by the window looking out over the little lane. It had got cooler during the morning, and the window of the cottage was misting up because of the steam from my coffee. An old-fashioned green four-wheel drive passed as I was sitting there, the driver in a dark jacket and a dog in the passenger seat barking at the world, but other than that I saw no one. Then I settled to a determined and thorough clean of the cottage, which was both satisfying and interesting. Although it was dusty this little place has obviously been well cared for. The paintwork is crisp and white now that I have washed it, the wooden stairs are shiny, and the glass in the windows must have been cleaned quite recently. Upstairs there is a big double bed (where Karl had slept) and a single bed, which is mine while I'm here. I re-arranged that room a bit, making it more homely, but there is nowhere to hang clothes and only one chest of drawers, which is full of bedding. It seems I will be living out of a suitcase for another week.

I had a brief panic when I realised that I was running out of shampoo. That was one thing we hadn't thought of at either supermarket, and in Texas I was using the stuff provided by the hotels. Then, in a high cupboard in the bathroom, I found shampoo, conditioner and some seriously expensive hand and body lotion. That set me wondering. I didn't think this cottage could be Karl's, it didn't have that feel about it, so whose is it? It isn't a commercial holiday let, because so much personal stuff is littered everywhere.

Probably the owner or the person who uses it most is in some way associated with my sort of community, because of the books … and the shampoo is a make that women buy. Does the cottage belong to a friend of Karl's? A woman friend, obviously. Somehow, though, I am not worried by not knowing. My life is in limbo until Karl comes back, and I am happy to let it be so. By the time the cottage was clean it was pitch dark and I cooked the mince and made some chilli and rice, then watched the news and ordinary, comforting British TV on my DeV until bedtime. I slept like a log.

Today I am going to explore beyond the cottage, but first I want to sit calmly in the Truth and hold all the people in my life to the Light. For the first time I understand why some people pray for those who have died. I wish I felt that there was something to be achieved in praying for Simon. All the ends of his life seem to be left untied. The best I can do, though, is to lift to the Creator this hunger I feel still to do something for Simon, to ease his passage, to tie up the ragged ends, to make the injustices right. Although I know he is dead, it is as if I cannot actually believe it to be so.

Friday 21ˢᵗ January 7.00am

I have been awake for hours but I wouldn't let myself get up. When I was teaching I sometimes had sleepless nights like this if I were worried about my work, about a student, or government inspectors, or in the last few years, about the increasing sense of being sidelined. Back then someone told me that it is better to lie in bed in the dark and rest, than to get up and do something, because the body still gains some benefit. I have never been convinced by that, but I do think it helps to keep my body in some sort of rhythm, especially now when, of course, I am still not over my jet lag.

I woke at about 2.00am. I had been having a really vivid nightmare, so vivid that it was not like a dream at all, and there was no part of it where odd things happened that don't happen in real life. It was really a remembering, but a remembering in my sleep. It

145

started with Maria and me being driven in the Norwegians' car to Chasserton. I could feel that same sick, suspended feeling. Then it skipped a bit, and the sleeping memory resumed as we waited to be led across to the execution chamber. It was like reliving the whole thing. I felt the air conditioning as we entered the viewing room, and the cool of the glass that separated us from Simon when I touched it. I could hear the journalists' conversation. And I couldn't hear Simon, who was talking, talking, and looking at us … Then I woke, bathed in sweat and shivering at the same time.

The cottage was bitterly cold, the heating goes off at night. I looked out through the little window by my bed at the meadows and the hills, and I thought of the beginning of the Bible, where the creation is first described. The words say that the Spirit of God was moving over the waters, before ever dry land was made. I have thought for a long time that there is a profound truth expressed there, that the Spirit moves over chaos, over the unformed, over the unresolved, and creates order, form and resolution. I sat in my bed looking at the shades of black outside, and asked the same Spirit to move over my chaos and to bring calm and resolution, and gradually my heartbeat returned to normal. Then, of course, I had to go to the bathroom, which meant turning on a light and going all the way down the steep stairs and to the frigid bathroom. When I got back into bed I was even colder, and although I have snug and cosy bedding it took me a long time to warm up again, and I didn't go back to sleep.

It is still dark, of course, but the heating came on at 7.00am as I got out of bed, so as I sit here I can hear things clicking and creaking as everything warms up. I have a pot of coffee in front of me, reflected in the window. Perhaps I will make a tray of breakfast and go back to bed in a little while, but I won't try unless I begin to feel sleepy. In the meantime I might as well write about yesterday.

There is not a lot to write, actually. Once I was up and dressed and had written this journal I thought I would see whether I could find any information about what is going on at home with the tent city, and whether there has been any more reporting about Simon's

146

death. I knew I had to be careful. There is nothing to link this DeV to me, but we know these things can be monitored and I have no idea whether anyone is looking for me. It seems Karl thinks so, and so I'm playing safe. First I went onto an ordinary news site and read about the signing of a trade agreement between the New Alliance and the Chinese. I read about a murder in the Caribbean (gang related), and about the boost to our economy brought about by the new gun laws. It seems that as a nation we have bought thousands of dollars worth of hardware and spent as much again at becoming proficient in using it. By the time the year is out there will be as many weapons in certain areas of England as there are in Chicago or Detroit. From that page I found a link to an editorial about the connection between poverty and gun possession, so I went to that page as any reasonably interested reader might. There seems to be a question of whether there even is a link, since in parts of the country it seems to be the middle classes who are embracing the new right to be armed. I cynically wonder if it is because they have more to lose from crime or civil disobedience? There was another link to an article about food banks, though, and from there I found a short article about homelessness and tent cities. Most of it was about America, but there were a couple of paragraphs about the growing number of encampments in England, and a picture of people sitting in Hyde Park with a posse of police standing behind them. I didn't really learn anything new, so I went back to the article about poverty and gun control, and clicked on a link to schooling, and which schools have come out best in the recent league. I was not remotely interested in that, but I thought that if anyone was monitoring the sites I accessed, perhaps it might suggest I was a family person. I left my DeV on that page while I made more coffee (the stuff we bought is not Fair Trade, but I must admit it is really good!) then clicked on a couple of reports on Oxfordshire schools, again to leave a false trail. Then I checked the weather forecast, and again did a detailed check on Oxfordshire. This is probably ridiculous, but it does no harm.

It was a crisp, cold morning yesterday. I had hoped to explore outside, around the cottage, so I put on Karl's jumper and my waterproof jacket, and headed out. The cottage is not, in fact, totally isolated. There is an ancient church one side of it, and a large cemetery behind the garden. Along the road, down in a bit of a dip, there is a row of old stone houses, but looking up the lane I could see nothing beyond the church because of the bend in the road. This cottage has no windows in the side walls, just in the front and back, so I wonder whether anyone in the little flint houses will even be able to tell that this cottage is occupied? I stood in the lane looking both ways before I locked the cottage door. Karl hadn't told me not to go out, and he knows me well enough to know that I wouldn't stay inside for a week unless it was absolutely necessary. Still, I felt a bit frightened, exposed even, standing in the lane. The cottage seems like a safe place, the way your bed feels safe when you are a child and you think there is a monster in the wardrobe. As long as you stay under the covers the monster can't get you.

I decided to turn left first, up the hill. The church looks as if it is very old and very large. It made me wonder. Was this part of Wales once more densely inhabited? Were there clearances, like the Highland clearances, at some point? I climbed the steps to the porch, but the door was locked and on the noticeboard were torn and stained notices dating back two years. I walked round the church yard and found, to my surprise, a pathway leading to a gate, and a large old house with smoke pouring out of a chimney, and shrubs cut into well trimmed shapes. It is the vicarage, I suppose, or it was originally. It looks out over the other side of the hill into which my cottage is built, and must having stunning views from the windows looking towards the opposite slopes. I wandered through the grave yard and looked at the inscriptions on the tomb stones. They mostly dated from the nineteenth and twentieth centuries, with only one or two more recent.

I returned to the road and kept going left. Over the brow of the hill the road dipped down between high hedges, a sunken lane, and then I reached a bridge across a fast flowing stream. It was then that I saw the four-wheel drive vehicle again. Of course, it could have been a different one, but I heard it coming before it rounded the bend, and stood back among the trees next to the stream to look, and saw the same dog sitting in the passenger seat again. The driver was wearing the same dark jacket as before and one of those tweed flat caps and looking straight ahead, but for a moment I thought I had seen his face before. I can't think where, and maybe it is just that he is a 'type'. I have noticed before that even nowadays in the different regions of the country you still find distinctive features. I suppose he is a local farmer. I think that farming here must be very different from the experience of Amy's agricultural friends, whose children go to fee paying schools and who drink good whiskey from north of the border!

Once over the bridge the road narrowed again, and it occurred to me that if a car drove past me in one of those single lane stretches of asphalt the driver would be bound to notice me, and might perhaps wonder who I am. It seemed not to be a very sensible risk to take, so I headed back the way I had come and was home in time for lunch. In the afternoon I finished the book about the American pioneer and started *Hard Times*, defrosted some chicken pieces and made a chicken stew, then watched an old detective programme, and started knitting my squares. I drew the curtains as soon as it started to be dusk, because I feel vulnerable and I didn't want anyone looking in. This is so unlike me. I usually love the dusk beyond the window panes, and at home I don't draw the curtains until it is really dark. I hope that when all this is over I will get my confidence back quickly.

I do feel sleepy now, although it is quite late to be going back to bed. Maybe I'll read upstairs over breakfast and see what happens.

Saturday 22nd January. 8.00am

I am really worried, worried to the point that I can feel my heart thumping in my chest, and my mouth is dry. I have just been outside, via the back door next to the bathroom, and I have seen something which definitely wasn't there yesterday: footprints in the flower bed right by the window, next to the holly bush where Karl

149

and I cut the holly on Wednesday. And that is just the latest scary thing.

Perhaps it isn't surprising that I slept so deeply when I went back to bed yesterday morning. It had been quite soothing writing this journal and I made decaffeinated coffee to go with the breakfast I took back to bed. *Hard Times* is interesting but quite slow, and the room upstairs was warm by the time I climbed back under the covers. I must have fallen into a deep sleep, because when I woke around eleven o'clock I couldn't think for a moment where I was. I thought I was in the hotel room at Stanley, and when I opened my eyes and saw the cotton print curtain hanging in front of my little window, I couldn't make any sense of it. Then I heard a sort of cracking noise downstairs and suddenly I remembered where I was.

Leaping out of bed, running across the room and skittering down the steep stairs as I did made me feel sick. I had got up much too quickly. Then I slipped on the third stair from the bottom and bruised my ankle. I stood at the foot of the stairs, my heart pounding, but I couldn't hear anything. I sat on the bottom stair and took a deep breath. Maybe I hadn't actually heard anything, I had been only half awake, after all. Or maybe it was a sound from outside. What could it have been? It had been a sort of wooden noise, a noise I vaguely recognised. Then I remembered, years ago when I was helping Amy and my brother who were renovating their first house, prizing the old skirting board away from the wall. It was that sort of noise.

I walked to the front door, which has a curtain over it to stop draughts. Then I froze again. Very close to me, just on the other side of the door, an engine started up. I looked sideways through the crack in the curtains, and saw the four-wheel drive as it moved away. There was no dog in the passenger seat this time, but in the brighter light of the morning I could see the green waxed jacket the driver was wearing. I have seen a jacket like that before.

Back upstairs I dressed quickly and put on outside shoes. I went quietly out through the back door, looking carefully all around me. That's how I know for sure there were no footprints on the flower bed yesterday. I walked round the side of the cottage to the lane and stood looking at the front door. There were scratches there, next to the heavy old lock. Had the door been scratched before? I honestly can't remember, although I think I might have noticed when I went out that way yesterday, and locked up.

I went back inside and sat shaking, not on my favourite chair by the window, but on the green wing chair by the little table, where nobody glancing in would see me. I desperately wanted to contact Karl but I know for sure I must not do that. I tried to reason with myself. For all I know the farmer in the Land Rover might own this cottage, but if he does, why would he try to break in? Had he tried to break in, or had the marks on the door been there all along? Was I sure that the vehicle being outside the cottage had anything whatsoever to do with me? After all the sheep in the field opposite must belong to someone, why not him? And, let me be honest, life has been fairly strange for the last ten days but actually, to the best of my knowledge, I have not broken a single law, I really shouldn't have anything to worry about. Probably I have read far too many novels in my life, and it is all too easy to lose touch with reality when you're jet lagged and living in total isolation, and when you have seen a murder, first hand, very recently. I began to calm down. I made some coffee and tuned into a talking radio station on my DeV. Actually, to my amusement, the only radio station I could find was Radio Dublin, the internet connection here seems to vary in strength, so I listened to a documentary about European immigrants settling on the West Coast of Ireland. It was by now midday, so I decided to knit until lunch time, knitting being a calming activity, and when I looked up, all I could see outside was winter sun on the hills, and sheep, and black birds swooping low over the marshland. Everything seemed so normal. I spent the rest of the day reading, knitting, watching TV on my DeV and cooking. I defrosted more mince and made three individual shepherd's pies, and I opened a bottle of wine after dinner and had a couple of glasses while I read *Hard Times* and a wind whistled around the cottage, making me feel warm and secure. I slept well.

And now this. I woke up feeling optimistic. It is already Saturday and Karl said he would take about a week to sort things out. I am actually quite happy on my own. I am in a sort of limbo, I cannot know what is going on at home with my friends, but I don't feel abandoned because I think Karl will somehow make it all right. He left on Wednesday, so the week is half over now, more or less. It is a bright, cold morning, and I thought that before I settled to this journal I would walk once round the garden, to see if any bulbs were coming through. It's what I would have done at home in the flat gardens, if I were there. And that is when I saw the footprint. Someone, a person wearing a boot with a heavy tread, has stood on the bare flower bed by the lobby window, right up close to the cottage, since I went out there yesterday.

Why would anyone do that? My mouth went dry and I came in at once, locking the back door. And here I sit, wondering what can possibly be going on.

Years ago when I was still teaching, the pastoral team was sent on a course that was supposed to introduce us to a certain sort of therapy which was very popular at the time. It was quite interesting, although I didn't use it much in my pastoral work afterwards because it required too much time to be spent individually with students, and of course I didn't have that time. Anyhow, one of the terms they used was 'catastrophising'. Catastrophising is something it seems we all do, it is when we allow our minds to run wild in the direction of catastrophes. For example, I used to catastrophise each time I was due for a performance management review in the last few years at work, when I was so badly out of step with the political direction in which education was going. I would start by thinking, "Pat is going to watch me teach. She has been upset with me ever since that occasion when I objected to George's suspension. She is bound to find fault with me." Then I would start to think, "I am a bit of a liability in this school now. If Pat gives me a low grade and I appeal, I don't think the Head will back me." Then I would start to think ahead. Would my position in the school become untenable? If I left, would I ever get another job? Probably not at my age and with my politics. So my pension would be affected, and pensions had by then already been severely reduced from the heydays of substantial retirement payouts. I would have to sell my house … and so on it would go. The thing about catastrophising is that it is a sort of mental panic. It is irrational. It looks ahead to things which may not happen. The way to deal with it is to force oneself to stand back and look calmly at the fears.

So now I am trying to do that. I need to think carefully about what is realistic and what is just panic, panic brought about mostly, I should think, by the succession of unexpected and really stressful things that have been happening, probably still combined by jet lag, although actually I don't feel jet lagged today.

Two things are causing this fear. The first, of course, is that I suspect that someone, the man in the Land Rover, tried to break in to the cottage yesterday morning. The second scary thing is that someone was peering in through the window at some point after I looked outside – probably sometime at night, I think. There is something else too, a sort of discomfort which I feel about the man in the four-wheel drive, something which makes me feel I can't trust him.

I will try to be rational. Do I actually know that he tried to break into the cottage? I was asleep and a noise woke me. Afterwards I thought it was like the noise of someone trying to prize wood away from stone, but can I actually be sure that is what I heard? Now I think about it, I can't. And do I know that the marks were not already there on the door, by the lock? Again, I don't think I can know that. So my fears about yesterday's scary moment are quite possibly totally unfounded.

Well, what about today? There certainly is a footprint in the flower bed (I have just gone outside to check again, in case I was somehow imagining it). So someone was standing there, and it is difficult to imagine any other reason for a person to be there, than to try to see in. The window there is small, no grown adult would attempt to climb in that way, and it is not close enough to the back door to reach through and unlock anything. The person must just

153

have been looking. Now that is odd, because the window at the back only provides light to the little lobby area, there is a solid plank door through to the living room and I keep it closed, for warmth. No doubt someone peering in would see light through the cracks of the door and under it, so he or she would know someone is here, but that is about all. Could it be a neighbour from one of the row of little houses further down the road? I always like to think that country people will be friendly, that a neighbour would call round openly to introduce himself or herself, but of course that might be a romantic view of the countryside. Perhaps the locals are suspicious of visitors? Perhaps there is bad feeling about English people owning cottages in Wales? Still, anyone wanting to know whether someone is staying here wouldn't need to peer in through the lobby window. The light shining through the curtains at the front would tell its own tale.

The more I think about it, the less it makes sense. I wonder if there is another much more innocent explanation? But I can't think of one…

I so wish I could talk to someone. I have been on my own since Wednesday and I'm catastrophising too easily! I think I probably need to do something physical and practical. There is no washing machine here, but I could usefully hand wash some of my clothes and dry them while it is so crisp and bright outside. Perhaps, too, I should go for a stroll down the lane towards the little stone terrace? Surely I won't seem suspicious to them if my washing is drying on an airer in the garden and I walk right past their houses? It should at least show that I have nothing to hide, and the fresh air will do me good. It really is a beautiful day.

Sunday 23rd January. 8.30am

I hope I am not becoming unstable. My sleep last night was riddled with bad dreams that seemed to muddle all the business of my life in one stressed, confused knot of anxiety. I can't remember it all, it made no sense, but at one point Fran and I were standing by the tent encampment about to start morning classes when the chaplain from Simon's prison appeared, accompanied by the head teacher from my school. I had a terrible feeling of dread. Then Maria was there, and Simon was sitting on one of the logs beside the camp fire, and a group of people from the flats was walking across the park towards us shouting. I woke to the white light of morning with my heart pounding and at once I realised something. It came over me like a dash of cold water. The man in the four-wheel drive reminds me of Derek, the guy I don't trust who has applied for membership.

Obviously it cannot be him. So now I am having to fight a new fear, the fear that so much oddness is making me lose all sense of perspective. I pulled open the chintz curtains and saw with surprise why the morning light was so bright: snow has fallen overnight and everywhere is covered with a thin veil of white. It is very pretty.

I got up at once and despite the cold of the bathroom I have had a bath and washed my hair with that luxurious shampoo. I have eaten scrambled eggs for breakfast and I have half the large pot of coffee on the windowsill in front of me. I know I have to take myself in hand. I need somehow to ground myself back into the calm normality of life. I have heard of people who have had traumatic experiences struggling to adjust back to everyday living and I'm sure (well, almost sure) that is all that is happening to me. I am a little ashamed. It is not as if I have been a refugee, or had to live through the sorts of problems they experience regularly in places like the Caribbean, or been fighting in a war. People who survive those sorts of things must be much tougher than me. I have always thought I was quite a strong person, but obviously not.

I am not sure how to do this. I am one of those lucky people who has always had friends around me and on a couple of occasions when I have had to face really difficult situations, like when DD died so suddenly, I have even gone to a counsellor. One way or another, I realise, I have always settled myself and worked things through by talking to people. Now I cannot. In a way this journal is supposed to serve the same purpose. I am talking to myself, or talking to God, but it seems less straightforward with nobody to answer. Well, maybe that is one of the lessons I need to learn from this peculiar period of my life. I will sit in silence and ask for the grace and the peace to be calm again, and rational.

Sunday 23rd continued. 5.30pm

I think today has been a really successful day. After my journal entry this morning I sat for a while, not trying to work things out in my head, but just asking the Spirit to order my heart and my mind. I sat by the window in full view of anyone who might be passing in an act of rebellion against my fears, looking out at the meadow across the lane and at the hills beyond, everything covered in a sprinkling of snow and sparkling in the sunlight. The white of the lane was unmarked by tyre tracks, but there were some sort of animal prints, tracing a path with deliberate paw steps along the other side of the road. As I sat there I felt a sort of optimism begin to creep into me. It started as a physical feeling, a sort of well-being, so that after sitting there not really thinking about anything more profound than how pretty everything is, I slowly became aware of how comfortable the chair was and how pleasant it is to sit with one leg crossed over the other. I was wearing Karl's snuggly jumper and I started to be aware of the softness of the wool. Then I began to think about how good my hair feels after using that lovely shampoo. The thoughts and feelings seemed to drift through my mind the way thoughts do when you're dozing off, but I felt wide awake and deeply content. I seemed to sit there for ages, but actually I realise that I had noted the time when I started to write my journal, 8.30am, and when I looked at my watch it was only just after 10.00am. I hadn't resolved anything, or had any fresh insights into my circumstances, but I felt as if my life had been set in order somehow.

I have spent the rest of the day really usefully. My washing was almost dry by the time I brought it in yesterday, and I found an iron in the cupboard under the ladder-like stairs (but no ironing board) so I pressed the jeans and the T-shirts using the table and they are ready to wear again. I watched an old movie about an American slave while I knitted two squares after lunch, and I explored the rocky slope between the church yard and the cottage, which was quite precarious because the snow has only melted where it has been in direct sunlight. There are still no tyre tracks in the lane, and definitely no footprints other than my own around the cottage, but I heard the sounds of children playing quite a long way away, and that seemed like a comfortable sort of noise. Now I am sitting by the black stove thinking what an unusual Sunday it has been, and working out that this time last week I was at the airport in Houston getting ready to fly home. There is a sort of motto in my community, 'Live adventurously' and I feel I am doing so! One of the shepherd's pies is defrosting in the kitchen and I will eat the last of the broccoli with it. With any luck Karl will be back in a couple of days.

Monday 24th January 9.00am

I was woken by a telephone this morning. It was such a surprise. I had seen that there is one of those old silver-coloured land line telephones upstairs in the cottage by the hub, but it hadn't occurred to me that it might work. Most people stopped using phones like that years ago. But then, they stopped using ovens like the one in the kitchen of the cottage too, but this one works really rather well! The phone had one of those old-fashioned ring tones, like something from a movie, and I sat up in bed and looked at it, wondering what to do. In the end I was still wondering when it stopped ringing. I looked at my watch: 6.45am. I pulled back the curtains and looked outside. There has been more snow overnight, thicker this time, resting in little heaps on the tops of the fence posts opposite. The heating was not on yet, so I snuggled down under the covers and wondered if I would go back to sleep.

Of course I didn't. I was perplexed about the phone. I can only think of two possibilities for why it would ring. One, the most likely, is that it was a wrong number. The other is that Karl is trying to contact me.

To be honest, I really don't think that is very likely. Although all the publicity in the early years of this century was about security forces tracing our mobile phone communications, land lines have always been vulnerable, even way back in the twentieth century. I also think that Karl would know I wouldn't answer it. How could I, with no VDU to tell me who is calling? It occurs to me now, that if this cottage still has a land line maybe other surrounding dwellings do too. Perhaps mobile phone reception is not very good here. That wouldn't be surprising, because who would build masts in an area so sparsely populated? And I know that internet connection comes and goes here, that was why I ended up listening to Radio Dublin the other day! In that case, if I'm in a community where lots of people still use land line codes, a wrong number is all the more likely. I am so glad I didn't answer it!

As soon as the heating started to click, that friendly warming-up sound, I pulled on Karl's jumper and came downstairs. There are mounds of snow on the windowsill at the front, and everything outside looks clean and white, but the sky is heavy and grey. This little room warms up quickly but it is a very cold day. While I was looking out of the window a tractor grumbled slowly by, leaving deep tread marks in the snow. The driver was a woman with a red woolly hat on her head. Life here is so very different from life at home! I think I will go for a walk when I have finished writing this entry.

I am very aware of how self-centred this journal has become. Somehow, living alone in this little remote place I feel as if the tent school, my community, my friends and Amy, are all very far away, almost as if they are in a different life. I have not really thought about what might be going on there for several days, and I've only thought of my friends when wishing I could talk to them about my life. How selfish can you get? I plan to spend some time now thinking of each in turn, mentally lifting them to the Light. It feels good sitting here, looking out at the snow (it has just started to drift down again, huge

158

flakes of snow blowing up the lane in the wind). Yesterday was a day for getting my own life in order. Today is a day for thinking of others.

Tuesday 25th January 7.30am

I really wish Karl would come back. On Sunday and yesterday morning I thought I had re-established a sense of calm in my life, I was beginning to feel like the person I had been before all this started, the person who worked in the charity shop and knitted squares for the nuns and did useful but unimpressive tasks for my community, and went to a book group. I even began to feel as if very soon now I would go back to that life. I thought of my flat, cosy and comfortable with its view across the park, and the river, and the market, all those familiar places where I have lived my ordinary life, and I longed for them the way sometimes I long for people. Then bit by bit yesterday I lost my calm again, and now I am frightened.

It was after 10.00am by the time I was putting on my shoes and jacket. I spent quite a long time thinking of the people in my life, then dressed and had eggs for breakfast again. It seemed right to fuel up before going out into the snow. I cleared up the kitchen, and then hunted high and low, and successfully, for a pair of gloves. I found them in the lobby, on a shelf above the garden tools, but they are not gardening gloves. They are a bit large for me, but that's no problem.

I love snow. Living in the south I almost never see any, so it has that magical quality associated with American Christmas movies or Charles Dickens. It was not falling so heavily by the time I let myself out by the back door, but the air met me with a blast of cold. I pulled my hood up over my head and, bracing myself into the wind, I set off down the lane. For a moment, as I rounded the corner of the cottage, I thought I heard the phone ringing again, but then I thought it was probably just the wind in some wires somewhere. Surely you wouldn't hear a phone ringing through those thick stone walls?

159

I did this walk a few days ago, on Saturday, the afternoon that I washed my clothes, but it looked quite different in the snow. The lane goes downhill away from the church, and after a wild, rocky stretch of bank there is the row of terraced houses. On Saturday I had it in mind that I was showing myself to my neighbours, indicating I had nothing to hide, but actually I hadn't seen anyone and if anyone saw me there was no indication of it. This time I was less bothered about the neighbours, and more interested in the business of walking in the snow in shoes which, though sensible, were never designed for this sort of weather. I did glance up once as I passed the last of the houses, and saw that there were lights behind net curtains in the front window, but that was the only sign of life.

On Saturday I had walked as far as a barn on the left of the road, and then turned back. I seemed to get there quite quickly this time so I decided to keep going. I felt a little as I feel when I travel on my own, for example the first time I visited Simon: daring and adventurous and independent. The road started to climb as it rounded a bend, and there were high banks on either side. I decided I would walk as far as a copse of trees on the right at the top of the slope, so I put my head down into the wind which kept changing direction, and just kept going. It was bitterly cold but it felt good to be out, and I felt healthy and strong. I realised I am over my jet lag and perhaps nearly over the initial shock of Simon's death. As long as I didn't walk on the tractor tread marks, which were still slippery despite the new snow that had fallen on top of them, my shoes gripped fairly well. My socks were wet, but I knew I had dry ones at home, and I was enjoying myself. I reached the copse in no time.

The view from up there was lovely. The bank had gone and the hedge beside the road was low. I must have been looking out in much the same direction as I look from the cottage, but I was further down the valley and facing more to the west. In front of me white meadows spread out towards the stream. It must be the same stream I had seen when I walked in the other direction. Scattered across the valley are little stone houses, each one with a tree or two beside it, and most with smoke coming out of tall chimneys. It seems like a sentimental thing to say, but it looked like a Christmas card. My breath made steam in the air as I stood there, and the wind made my face burn. It was glorious.

And then I heard, in the distance, the sound of a helicopter. We hear them often at home, they are used to patrol the motorway (it is called EI3 now, English Interstate 3, instead of the M3, in order to bring 'cohesion' between all the members of the New Alliance). It was the first I had heard here, though, and it sounded wrong, alien, in this remote and snowy landscape. Without really thinking I moved into the little copse and stood up against a tree. I'm not sure why, it isn't as if I thought at that moment that anyone was searching for me, it was just a sort of instinct born of all that has happened recently. I found myself thinking that my footsteps will lead directly from the cottage to the place where I was standing, and wondering whether people in helicopters can pick up that much detail. I wasn't carrying my DeV so I couldn't be tracked that way ... then I realised that I was moving swiftly back into paranoid mode and I needed to be careful. I didn't move away from the tree, though.

The helicopter flew much closer, then directly overhead. It was black, or so it seemed against the dark grey sky as I peered up through the bare branches of my tree. It flew on to the other side of the valley, turned, followed the line of the river up hill and then flew back, seeming to follow the line of the lane. My heart was in my mouth as it flew directly overhead again, but the helicopter didn't slow down, just followed the line of the lane as far down the valley as I could see, and gradually the noise of it faded away.

I stood in the copse in the heavily falling snow and I could feel myself sweating and my heart pounding. Was someone looking for me? Who and why? Or was I once again catastrophising? If the authorities find helicopters useful for patrolling blocked motorways, presumably they also find them useful for patrolling other places which are inaccessible? Perhaps some walkers have failed to arrive at their destination and the emergency services have been called to search for them? Perhaps they routinely patrol in snowy weather because of children playing on the steep valley slopes, the way that helicopters patrol beaches in the summer? Or they could just have been out on a practice run.

I turned back into the lane and retraced my steps, but all the joy of walking in the snow and the cold was gone. It was snowing harder too, whirling round my ears, and my hood kept blowing down, so that I felt very exposed to the bitter cold. It seemed to take a long time to get back to the cottage, and all the while I could feel that partly submerged panic that comes from being out of control.

The cottage felt wonderfully warm when I finally got home, and it smelt good, a mixture of expensive shampoo, good food and some spray cleaner I had found in the lobby. I put the kettle on and made some lunch. I toasted cheese on bread, which added further to the delicious smells, and read *Hard Times*, and tried to convince myself that all was well. It was Tuesday, and Karl has been away a week. It is reasonable to expect him any time now.

Then a wonderful thought occurred to me. What if it were Karl in the helicopter? I am sure he would have access to that sort of transport, and he has said he will look out for me. I was beginning to feel really quite positive. I had eaten my lunch and drunk some hot chocolate. I was wearing dry socks and the cottage felt snug. Outside it was half dark although it was the middle of the day, and the snow was falling heavily, like a curtain, so that everything on the other side of the lane looked shadowy. I had that safe, cocooned feeling again. I decided it was time to do some knitting.

And then the phone rang again. It is upstairs and I was downstairs. I just froze. I have been here a week without it ringing and now it had rung twice in a day. I put the ball of wool down and went upstairs. I just looked at the phone. In cartoons when one of those old phones ring the handset jumps up and down in the cradle, but of course in real life that does not happen. The ringing noise came from it, but otherwise it looked totally inert, dead, like a museum item. At last it stopped ringing.

I turned to the little window that looks out at the back of the cottage, over the lobby extension. The land back there is rough. It seems someone once had a garden there but all that is left now are some scattered shrubs and some paving stones. Perhaps it is full of bulbs in the spring time. The roof over the lobby slopes. It is rather unattractive, actually, made of some sort of corrugated metal, but in the snow it looked elegant. Then I saw – there was a sort of indentation in the whiteness, as if in one place the snow had been brushed off, and hadn't accumulated to the same depth as on the rest of the roof.

At once my heart started pounding again. I didn't think, as was most likely, that a cat had been on the roof, or that heat from the lobby had caused some snow to melt. I didn't think that sometimes snow just slips off roofs for no apparent reason. I didn't even think that I might be imagining the dent in the snowline. The light was very bad after all. I just knew, with a lurch of my stomach, that I was being watched. It was illogical. It might even be crazy, but there the feeling was, and it was accompanied by a feeling of certainty that all is not well.

And the phone started to ring again. I didn't know whether to scream or laugh. In the end I sat on the floor by the table and cried. I don't think I have ever felt so lost in my life. And then I went downstairs and knitted squares, and listened to something on my DeV about freak waves, and felt a weird disconnected feeling, as the world outside got darker and colder.

Wednesday 25th January 6.00am

It is bitterly cold in here but I am already up and dressed, wearing my warmest t-shirt like a vest, a cotton blouse and Karl's thick woollen jumper. I have hard-boiled the remaining eggs and packed them in an old take-away container, along with the rest of my bread and a plastic carton of milk. I have three apples left which I will take. I have dry socks because these shoes are not waterproof and I think it is probably dangerous to get wet, cold feet if I am out for any length of time. This backpack is not designed for mountains and snow, it was just a fashionable high street purchase bought a couple of years ago because it went well with a jacket, but I have put everything in plastic bags to keep dry. Just as I was coming downstairs I saw the torch which is kept, I assume in case of power cuts, on a shelf on the tiny landing. I checked it worked, and put it in the outside pocket, then picked up some matches. It is still dark, and it is still snowing, which I am glad about. I have the last of the mince heated up on my plate and when I have eaten it, I plan to go. I'm hoping the snow will drift and cover my tracks, although I am not quite sure yet in which direction to head.

Yesterday was a strange day. The snow turned into a real blizzard. Well, actually I don't really know what the proper definition of a blizzard is, but the snow was heavy, huge flakes falling fast and swirling in the wind. Sometimes, if gusts blew towards the front of the cottage, the snow sounded almost like hail on the windows, but at other times it seemed to drift and float, as if the flakes had no intention of ever landing. The wind moaned in the chimney. The lane was covered in a smooth, undulating layer of white, and I couldn't see the hills.

I suppose I had gone into some sort of psychological overdrive on Monday afternoon – or perhaps I short-circuited emotionally. I sat by the black electric heater with the lamp by my left shoulder to make good light for my knitting. Methodically I knitted three squares, starting in the corners and increasing then decreasing. One was white, made of some sort of soft baby wool, one was flecked like tweed, in greys and greens, and the third was a bright, alarmed red. About every fifteen or twenty minutes the phone rang, but I ignored it. By three thirty it was almost dark outside because of the storm and I drew the curtains and continued with my red square. By five the cottage was beginning to feel cool. The heating was still working but it must have been very cold outside. I put on an extra layer under Karl's jumper and made hot drinks at intervals until about 7.00pm. I decided to eat then, and took out the third shepherd's pie from the freezer.

I'm not sure I was being very sensible, although really, under these circumstances, what does 'sensible' mean? I had no idea if I genuinely had anything to fear. On the one hand, Karl obviously thought I needed to be careful, although he also seemed to think he could sort it out, whatever 'it' is. On the other hand I live in one of the oldest democracies in the world, a country where human rights are respected and protected. What did I really think was going to happen? Yet somehow I couldn't make my mind settle to calm common sense. If only the phone would stop ringing. If only Karl would come back.

It was only yesterday morning that it occurred to me that perhaps, after all, it genuinely was a wrong number. We were – are – in the middle of a very big storm, probably a once-in-a-decade event, and friends and relatives would phone each other, in these outlying areas, to make sure all was well. That would explain why the phone only started ringing on Monday, when the bad weather approached, and perhaps it would explain why it didn't ring last night. I had been dreading the thought of lying there hearing the phone every ten or fifteen minutes, but the last call came just after nine in the evening. I didn't sleep well, of course, I was cold to add to all my other problems, and I had vague and threatening dreams, but at least I wasn't disturbed by all that ringing.

I have noticed before that sometimes a sort of calm and rationality follows a bad night. When I was teaching it would sometimes happen that I would lie awake half the night worrying about something at work, but in the morning, when I should have felt ragged and exhausted, I would feel organised and ready to act. My thought that the phone calls could just have been friendly neighbours checking up was typical of those sorts of non-panicky moments. The day was made even better by the fact that the phone didn't start ringing. I decided that I was expecting Karl's return any time, and I could usefully clean the cottage again. For a while the snow stopped although the clouds stayed low and threatening. I thought Karl couldn't come yet, the roads would probably be impassable, but I wanted to be ready. I had a useful morning washing floors, spraying furniture and hoovering rugs, and felt weary but reasonably content at lunch time.

As I sat knitting after my cheese and biscuits (I only had one portion of cheese left) and looking at the light snow which had begun to drift down again, I started to think about the last few days. I felt I had created a web of panic from a series of events which were really non-events: a footstep in the flower bed (well, that was odd), a helicopter flying over, a man wearing a green wax jacket like Derek, the green-jacket man, and a phone that had rung several times – well, lots of times! I know from writing to Simon that if people are on their own too much their thoughts can get out of hand. Probably, I thought, that was what had been happening to me. People need people, we are made that way, and I have lived the greater part of my life in an electronic world where there is always someone at the other end of a DeV or an old fashioned computer or phone.

The cottage seemed a little warmer yesterday afternoon, I wished there were an outdoor thermometer because it is really hard to judge from one's own senses – after all, I had spent the greater part of the morning cleaning and my blood felt as if it were rushing around my body. I finished yet another square, they take me about forty minutes on average, and decided to read some more of *Hard Times*. I felt pleasantly sleepy and still rational and calm. In fact, I think I might even have dozed off, sitting snugly beside the black heater.

Until the phone rang again. It was just getting dark, the grey sky outside turning to a purple- black, the snowflakes catching the light streaming out from the cottage window. My rationality seemed to vanish with the first ring. My heart started to pound, my mouth went dry, I felt almost sick.

Well, if I wanted to keep my sanity, I thought, I needed to answer that phone. When I had spoken to the kindly neighbour, either helpfully checking on the visitor in the cottage, or meaning to phone Great Aunt Edna but getting the last digit wrong, I would feel much better. I was making trouble for myself, causing myself to panic, by my persistent inaction. I put my book to one side and stood up – and the ringing stopped.

I went upstairs, drew the curtains and stood by the phone. It was lovely and warm up there, warmer than downstairs although I had left the door at the foot of the stairs closed to keep the heat in. I didn't have to stand there for long. I allowed the phone to ring a couple of times. I didn't want to give the impression I had been waiting for it. Then I picked up the receiver.

"Hello," I said, in what I hoped was a calm, neutral voice.

There was a silence at the other end.

"Hello?" I said again. "Can I help you?"

Again there was a silence, then a male voice said, "Possibly. Who am I speaking with, please?"

'Speaking with', not 'speaking to' – a North American turn of phrase. Not a local, then…

"Can I help?" I asked again. I had no intention of giving away any more information than necessary.

"I'm trying to locate a friend," the voice said. "Who am I speaking with?"

"Who are you looking for?" I countered.

"Just a friend," the voice said. "I'm troubled for her – I think she might be in danger."

My heart was pounding and my mouth felt dry. "Yes, the weather is awful, isn't it?" I agreed, although I was sure that wasn't what he meant. "But wherever your friend is, if she is warm and dry, that is something. Where are you phoning from?"

"Being warm and dry isn't everything," my caller said, and now I thought I could definitely hear a mild American accent behind the apparently BBC English. "I hope that by the morning my friend will be somewhere where nobody thinks to look for her – nobody who means her any harm."

"Goodness!" I said, pretending not to understand – not knowing if I did understand. "Who could wish harm on your friend?"

"You'd be surprised," the voice said, and the line went dead.

I stood by the phone for ages. After a while I started to wonder if I could find out where the call had come from. DeV phones all have caller display, and I remember when I was younger and we had independent mobile phones and cordless land lines, they also had little VDUs. This phone pre-dated that sort of technology, but I had a feeling a person could phone some number to find out where the last call had come from. I thought perhaps if I lifted the phone I would get a menu. Anyhow, it seemed worth trying, so I lifted the receiver.

The line was absolutely dead. There was no hum, no old-fashioned 'engaged' sound, nothing. I jiggled the cradle the way they do on old movies. Nothing. I put the receiver down and lifted it again. Nothing. I even shook the phone. It made a light jangling sound, but that was all. It was absolutely dead.

Common sense said that the storm must have brought down the lines. I didn't believe it for a minute.

I went downstairs in a daze. That disconnected feeling had taken over again, even more than before. I realised I needed to find out what was happening across the country. Of course, if I had been watching the news on my DeV I would probably have known of the approach of the storm. I would have heard Fox News' warnings about not travelling if it could possibly be avoided, about looking out for elderly neighbours. For the first time I wondered whether the storm extended even to Hampshire. What else had been happening that I knew nothing about? Keeping away from electronic communication was all very well, but I suddenly felt I really needed to know what was happening. Karl had bought me this little device, he obviously expected I would use it sometimes and I had watched films and listened to the radio on it, until I became so frightened. I was probably being unnecessarily cautious... I turned on my DeV and waited for it to come to life. The signal was poor – all things considered I'm surprised I had a signal at all, but after a few minutes I was able to go on line and I started surfing the news channels.

Cymru-Fox had the clearest news bulletin. The others kept breaking up, even Cymru-Fox came and went a little, but I caught a weather update that showed the storm sweeping right across England and Wales. Trees are down, power lines are cut, a woman in Hertfordshire gave birth to twins in the back of an ambulance trying to get to the hospital on the American base (mother and baby boys doing well) and there were pictures of American GIs digging old age pensioners out from a care home outside Cardiff.

I almost turned the DeV off then – despite my determined rationality I was very mindful of the danger of being tracked – but I thought I'd just catch the rest of the news. So I kept it on.

And I saw Jo on the screen. Jo, with her hands behind her back and with ATTF officers either side of her, and with Claire behind her in the crowd, holding Jamie and crying. Jo, with her hair standing up at the back of her head as if she had been brought straight from her bed. Jo, with a strange look on her face which was not resignation, but wasn't hope either … The warm Welsh voice told us that in the south of England anti-terrorist forces had raided a number of houses and had arrested a total of thirteen suspected agitators who were to be questioned under the new Homeland Security legislation.

I turned the DeV off and sat there, stunned. So Karl had been right, there were – are, real threats. If I had been at home, no doubt I would have been arrested too. By bringing me here Karl had saved me – for the time being. But there was that phone call – what did it mean? It could have been someone phoning on behalf of Karl, in which case I was being warned – I needed to leave the cottage. Or it could be some trick of the ATTF which Karl knew nothing about, maybe a Welsh part of the organisation checking their information. But would they warn me like that? Or would they perhaps want me to run away in the middle of the worst storm in years, in this remote area, to die of exposure and be found stiff and cold, a silly holiday maker ill-prepared and ill-equipped for a Welsh winter, no investigations needed, no conspiracy suspected…?

I decided I needed to go, the cottage is no longer safe. But going at that time – it was early evening by then – would be crazy. And I had nowhere to go. I have explored up and down this lane. I have seen the terrace of cottages, I have seen a barn which might not be locked, but which might be completely inaccessible, and I have seen a church and a rectory, which might no longer be a rectory. I needed to leave under cover of darkness – that seemed obvious – but I needed to protect myself from the bitter night-time temperatures. I decided to spend the next hours preparing and to make my escape first thing in the morning, before dawn.

I also realised that I needed to act as if I were not going to leave. Probably the cottage was being watched, or at least, I was wise to assume so, but all anyone could see from the outside was when the lights were on and off, and when I used the bathroom, so whatever preparations I made, I needed to give the impression that this was just an ordinary night.

For the first few days here I had not been pulling down the frayed old blind in the kitchen. Except to make a hot drink at bedtime I didn't go into that part of the cottage once my main meal was finished, but as the weather had grown colder I had started closing everything that would close, including the blind. That was good, I could prepare in there without anything seeming unusual from the outside. When I went into the kitchen at the time I normally go to bed, as well as putting on the kettle I put a pan of water on one of the slow-heating rings of the cooker, ready to hard-boil the remaining eggs. I packed my backpack at the time I would normally be upstairs getting ready for bed, and I turned my light out at pretty much my normal time. And then I lay there, waiting for the time to pass.

It was probably at about midnight or just after that I realised how little settling in the Light I had attempted over the last few days. I have written this journal, and I have intended to think of others and to let the Spirit rule my life, but it seems that no sooner do I achieve some level of calm than something else happens to knock me off balance. On Monday I had resolved, "Today is a day for thinking of others" but had I? First there had been the helicopter then the phone, and the truth is I have not been thinking of Jo and Fran, of the tent school, of my community, or even of Amy. And all that time they have been suffering – what? Arrest, interrogation, house searches? And Sabina and Imran were deported... Of course I couldn't sleep – the thought that I was about to leave the cottage in just a few hours was frightening and made me jittery. In a way I wanted to go at once. I held back the curtain a little and saw that it was still snowing, but in a lazy, sleepy sort of way, and I could see the moon behind some wispy cloud. I decided to try to sit in the Light for a while. I wrapped my duvet round me and sat on my bed in the dark. I was too neurotic – or too careful, to draw back the curtain so that I could look out over the snowy hills, instead I concentrated on sound.

There are lots of ways people find helpful to settle themselves in the Light. A number of people in my community concentrate on their breathing. Others go through a sort of 'letting go' exercise where they think about each limb and consciously relax it. I like to think of something separate from myself. My faith may not be orthodox but I believe in a loving power outside me, I don't want to concentrate on anything to do with myself and my ego. It is all too easy to be self-centred – it is a thing I battle against. I very often settle myself by looking at beautiful natural things: sky, water, leaves or flowers. Sometimes I think of a verse of poetry, often from the Bible. Last night I listened to sounds, and felt something in myself easing at once. I know that Muslims like to declare an intention before they do something to serve Allah, they know that it is the heart and not the action which really counts, and I think all these settling techniques are just the way we declare our intentions.

I could hear very little at first. There were tiny sounds that came from the fact that I was sitting on the bed – a slight squeak of the wooden frame as I moved one foot, a little whistle as I breathed out. The duvet has a crisp cotton cover that makes the sound of a gentle breeze if I touch it in a certain way. But mostly what I heard was stillness – no birds, no animals, no sounds of human life – nothing. I started to think about the first chapter of Genesis, the poem in which the Spirit of God moves over the surface of the uncreated world, and day by day, miracle by miracle, creates the earth. It has always been important to me, reminding me that Goodness creates only goodness: creates goodness out of chaos and disorder. I found it easy, then, to hold Jo in the Light, asking for something positive, something amazing, to come out of her arrest and interrogation. I thought of Sabina and Imran. Where would they be? I asked for great things to happen in their lives, for their love and generosity to find outlets wherever they have been sent. These things all seemed possible, even likely, in the stillness of the night. Somewhere a long way away I heard a rare sound – an owl hooting, and the beams of the cottage groaned a little in the cold. The world seemed very big, my life and all my fears and concerns seemed very small and really rather irrelevant. The next thing I knew it was after 4.00am, I had cramp in my right foot and my shoulders were cold. I climbed properly into the bed fully clothed and slept for another hour.

And now here I am – it is nearly 7.00am. In fact, as I write this the gentle clicking sounds of the heating coming on have just started. I will leave by the back door and head across the old cemetery behind the cottage, where a footpath seems mostly to be sheltered by trees. I don't know where it leads but I don't think the lane will serve my purpose. I really can't imagine what is going to happen next.

Wednesday 26th January. 5.30pm

I am very frightened.

I am sitting on the floor behind the altar of the church, not ten minutes' walk from the cottage, although it took me all day to get here.

I think I am pretty much at the end of the road and I still have no real idea what is going on.

Thank goodness I brought this torch, although it flickers quite a lot.

Thank goodness I brought food.

I am so cold.

Of all places, you would think that in a church I would feel the presence of the Spirit, that I would know I was being cared for. I feel only cold and – despite the change of socks – damp.

The helicopter hasn't flown over since it got dark but there are a few vehicles in the lane again.

I wonder if anyone can see this torchlight through the old, dirty stained glass windows?

I wonder if this will be my last entry?

Thursday 27th January 9.15am

People talk about all-time lows. I think I hit an all-time low last night. I was so tired, and so cold, and this church is grimy and unwelcoming. But now it is the morning, and I am still here, and as far as I can tell there are no more vehicles moving in the lane. Perhaps, after all, I am safe.

It was ridiculous, leaving the cottage as I did with no plan about where to go, although I really had no choice, and as it turns out it is a good thing I did.

When I left yesterday morning the first thing that struck me when I got outside was the feel of the air. It is hard to describe, but when I walked down the lane to the copse in the snow the air seemed wet and blustery, as if it had a life of its own. Yesterday morning it felt crisp and sharp. Flakes of snow were still drifting down but delicately, and I could see the lightness of clouds against deep black in the sky. I turned left then right from the back door, so that I was on the footpath leading up the hill behind the cottage, towards the old cemetery.

I was worried about footprints, especially if the snow stopped, but the wind had caused such drifting that I was able to walk on dry stone in some places – and anyhow, there was nothing I could do about it. The path took me around the outside of the graveyard, past a kissing gate for people who wanted to go towards the church, and then away to the left again, across a meadow. In places the snow was very deep, soon the turn-ups of my jeans were covered in sticky ice, and were wet and cold. It was very dark, the darkness before the dawn, but even so when I got to the hedge on the other side of the

173

field and looked back, I could see my footsteps in the snow. I turned by the hedge and walked up towards the top of the hill in the shadow of low-growth evergreens which were replaced by dry stone walling a little further along. I had not been out of the cottage for an hour, but I realised that I had already lost the footpath. Well, it didn't really matter, it was not as if I were going anywhere special.

When I came to a junction of stone walls I chose to take the one which would lead me further up the hill. I only partly thought it through. The higher I was, I felt, the more likely I was to see someone approaching. It started to get light and I realised that there was an unexpected benefit to walking right by the walls – the snow had drifted as it had when I set out, with deep piles in some places and exposed ground in others, and I was leaving few footprints.

It took me a while to reach the top of the hill. It was 11.22am when I stopped and drank some of the milk, and ate an apple. I sat in the shelter away from the wind, which also meant that I wasn't looking out towards the valley where the cottage is, but in the other direction. I was quite warm because of the exercise although my feet were cold and wet, and as I ate I felt something tickling my nose. I looked up and saw, to my delight, that it was snowing again – not as hard as it had in the last few days, but steadily, and with a breeze. There was a chance yet that my tracks would be covered.

The Cymru-Fox weather announcer had spoken of the unpredictability of our climate nowadays, and of the chance that the storm would veer north. It seems it had not. The sky darkened and more snow fell steadily, slanting north west in apparently random gusts.

I stood up and continued walking. It was harder now because of the wind, and I needed to keep my head down. My shoes were soaking, and kept slipping on the frozen ground, and my hood kept blowing off my head. I had seen no one since I left the cottage, the only signs of life were streams of smoke from the chimneys of the distant farm houses, and my view of them was limited now that the snow had set in again. I followed the wall as it climbed steadily upward until I came to a place where a stile intersected it, and a broken sign pointed in two directions. At last I paused and looked around me. I was close to the top of the hill, and if the weather had been good I suspect the view might have been amazing. To my left as I sat on the stile was the valley I was less familiar with, the valley the old rectory faces, the valley behind the cemetery. To my right was 'my' valley, the one the front of the cottage looked out onto, although I was further along now, closer to the place where my first walk had taken me, looking down towards the bridge that crossed the river. It occurred to me that I might be very visible sitting on the windy stile and I climbed down again, and started to try to think about what to do next.

To be honest I was actually feeling quite good at that moment. I had been walking steadily all morning and the physical energy had perhaps helped to work off some of my pent-up anxieties. I felt quite optimistic – I realised that I could see if anyone was approaching the cottage from this exposed position, and it occurred to me for a happy moment or two that any time now I might see Karl's car. Of course, I might not – and common sense told me that it was one thing to feel good in the early afternoon, after a hot breakfast and a good snack, and while it was still light. Soon it would start to get dark, and although we are well past the shortest day, the nights are still long and grim, and I needed to find somewhere where I would be protected from the storm. I looked around again. Visibility was closing in as the snow drove harder in a strengthening wind. Earlier I had been able to see several farmhouses on the surrounding valley slopes, but now I could only see one. Dared I go to their door and ask for accommodation? But what could I say, how could I explain myself? They would think I was mad. They would call the police. That was no answer at all.

On the other hand, where there are farms there are often barns. If I headed towards the one smoking chimney I could still see, wouldn't I find an outbuilding where I could shelter? But I thought of rural crime and people locking their sheds, and I thought of farm dogs, and it seemed too great a risk.

I had only been still for a few minutes at that point, and already

I could feel my body temperature dropping. The wind was bitterly cold and my feet and ankles were wet. There was a hole in the finger of one of the gloves too, and the gloves were wool, and were also wet … I hunkered down in the shelter of the wall and tried to think.

A car was indeed approaching along the lane. I heard it first, it was not electric, but then I saw it. It was a Land Rover. It was coming up from the bottom of the valley – I first saw it passing the terraced cottages, and then it reached 'my' cottage. And stopped.

From where I was of course I couldn't see the front of the cottage – in fact, all I could see was the roof, the one little window which looks out this way, the sloping corrugated iron extension for the lobby, and the patch of land behind. I had no idea what the driver was doing. I peered through the snowy air and for a while – it seemed like ages – nothing happened. The cottage hardly showed up in the landscape. Its roof was white but the stone chimney was only partly snow-covered. I kept my eyes on it, and wished I could see more. After a while a figure walked round the corner into my line of sight. At that distance I couldn't identify him – I wished it would be Karl but I didn't think it was. The person went up to the cottage where I couldn't see him – I supposed he was checking the door. I had locked it as I left. Then the figure reappeared, standing further back, looking up at the little upstairs window. As I watched I saw him jump, grasp something and slither up onto the sloping lobby roof. So I hadn't been imagining it when I thought someone had been there! He seemed to lie flat and to fiddle with the window. It is tiny, and I thought no grown adult would be able to get in that way. Then he slithered back down taking a shower of snow with him, and was gone. The Land Rover didn't drive away for quite a long time after that, though.

I stayed crouching behind the wall, and my teeth started to chatter. I hadn't got very far before someone came looking for me, but far enough – and I hoped the signs of the route I had taken were rapidly being obliterated by the weather. Now that the Land Rover had gone, it was always possible that if I didn't turn on any lights or give away signs that I was there, I could go back to the cottage at nightfall. It seemed like a risk, though. Yet I needed to go somewhere…

I was still thinking about it when the Jeeps arrived.

There were five of them. In that sort of storm it is really difficult to see colours. This is new to me, a person who has always lived, so to speak, inside, and in the south where storms like this one hardly ever happen. The world was white and grey and black, and the Jeeps were black, and so were the men who jumped out of them. They parked in a long row up the hill from the cottage in my clear line of sight, and I counted fifteen men, although there may have been more. I heard shouting, although the wind seemed to tangle the voices so that the sounds made no sense to me. At once a dozen or so men seemed to surround the cottage. There was more shouting, the sound of smashing glass, and then silence. Next I saw men gathering on the waste land behind the cottage. They stood in a circle. I thought they were holding guns but perhaps that was my imagination. I certainly didn't hear any shots at all. Then they scattered, some walked down the lane – I assume they were checking the terraced cottages, or perhaps looking to see if I were hiding somewhere nearby, and others towards the church.

Then a helicopter appeared. I didn't hear it before I saw it – some trick of the wind, perhaps, but there it was, following the line of the river down the valley, just as it had before. Now I was really frightened. There was no shelter around me. I was hidden from the men in the lane by the stone wall, but that would not protect me from someone flying overhead. I looked down at my clothes – blue jeans (ridiculous clothing for this sort of escapade), a black jacket with a hood, black shoes. It occurred to me that if I lay right by the wall, facing down and with my hood over my head, I might not be visible after all. The snow had drifted high on the cottage side of the wall but there was bare rock where I was crouching – and how much, after all, could anyone see in this weather? My backpack, however, is brightly coloured – I would need to lie on it. Quickly I put this plan into action, stretching out close to the wall, looking down at the rock, with my hood covering my head. And there I waited.

177

It was a strange and frightening sensation. I could hardly hear the sounds made by the men at the cottage, lying as I was behind the wall, with my hood over my head and the wind whistling and roaring around me. For a little while the helicopter seemed to fly further away, but if it were to follow the same route as last time it would come back up the valley on my side. For a minute or two I couldn't hear it at all, then the low rumble of engine and rotary blades returned and grew steadily closer.

I had no idea whether or not I was visible. The rock on the lee of the wall was dark and cold, but I couldn't make myself small enough to avoid lying on some snow. On the other hand, I also didn't know if the snow might be settling on me. I lay still, my heart pounding. The helicopter noises grew louder and louder. It seemed to me that it was circling around right overhead. I suddenly thought that my breath might be steaming in the air, giving me away, and I tried to move my head further into my folded right arm to shield my nose. Then the helicopter started to move away.

I lay very still. I could hear the howling wind and I was bitterly cold. The stones underneath me were slate and in one place my jeans had ridden up over my ankle, so that snow was falling on bare skin between my jeans cuff and my sock. My teeth started chattering, but still I dared not move. It was beginning to grow darker, either because of the storm or because evening was approaching. My spirits started to sink.

Then I heard the sounds of vehicles in the distance. There were no helicopter noises. Warily and stiffly I lifted myself up so that I was once again crouching behind the wall. I peered over. It was a bleak sight, a white landscape, driving snow and fading light, but as I watched first one and then a second Jeep started to drive away. I stayed where I was, and waited. There was still no helicopter and then another Jeep drove off, this time in the other direction. There was a strange yellow gleam in the west. It must have been sunset. Then, to my joy, the last two Jeeps left. I was alone again.

I waited for what seemed like quite a long time. I burrowed into my back pack and found the boiled eggs. I ate two, and feeling confident that there was now nobody around to see the evidence of my existence, I drank some coffee. The yellow gleam faded and the grey of the sky darkened to navy. There were no sounds of any other human. I could no longer see the one remaining farmhouse.

It seemed like time to move on – but where?

I stood, the wind buffeting me and tugging at the hood of my jacket, which just would not stay up. It was rapidly getting darker, and I needed to make some decisions. I tried to be logical. I had more or less decided earlier that looking for shelter at the farm was too much of a risk. I thought the terraced cottages represented an unknown factor too. I had been in 'my' cottage since last Tuesday and nobody had approached me, which meant I had no reason to think those people might be friendly. In addition, I had no idea what, if anything, had passed between the men from the Jeeps and the locals. It seemed reasonable to suppose that the inhabitants of the cottages might have been asked to report if they saw or heard anything unusual … So that ruled out those homes. I was left with three possibilities: the rectory, from which I had seen smoke coming when I first explored, 'my' cottage or the church itself.

I'm not sure how it worked in Wales, but in England all these big old church houses were sold, way back, I suppose in the 1970s. In Hampshire they are owned by people like Amy's friends, and some have been made into free schools or prep schools. They usually have smart cars parked on gravel drives, and wrought iron gates. However, and here I felt a little lurch of hope, they often also have beautifully kept outbuildings: potting sheds, summer houses, even children's treehouses. At one such old rectory not far from home there is a beautifully painted gypsy caravan in the elegant garden. People who live in houses like that often keep dogs, they like to walk them and throw sticks for them, but they are not working dogs. At night they stay inside, sleeping on beds besides kitchen ranges … It seemed to me that my best bet was to explore the old rectory outbuildings.

My sense of direction is not usually particularly good but I had spent an uncomfortably long part of the afternoon in one place, and I had got my bearings. I thought that to reach the rectory I needed to follow the slope of the hill back down as if I were heading for my cottage, but staying more to the left. It was very cold but no longer actually snowing by then, and I felt safest close to the wall, so although I suspected it was taking me too far up the valley, I followed the wall from the stile, and hoped it was the right direction.

After quite a short walk I realised I could smell something new. I stood still and sniffed again, it was the welcoming scent of wood smoke. I realised then that I was actually quite close to the rectory, although staring into the deep dusk all I could detect was a small clump of trees ahead and to the right of me. I stayed by the wall and kept walking, listening out for anything unusual or threatening: the bark of a dog, the sound of a car engine, or the sounds of voices. All I heard was the wind, which made a different noise now that I was close to the trees. I kept walking, slowly and carefully, trying to ignore the intense cold. Then I realised that I was approaching a place where the stone wall stopped and a hedge started. I was higher up the valley than the rectory, bearing down on it from a new angle, but now I could see it, darker against the dark sky, a block of shadow against the snowy ground.

There was a small road or track which I had not noticed when I last spotted the rectory, and an open gate like a farm gate, slightly tilted as if the hinges might be broken. I walked up the drive. There were lights behind curtains in two downstairs windows, and a high upstairs window which may have had frosted glass in it. There were no vehicles parked outside but there were tyre marks in the snow leading to the double garage doors. Next to the garage was a single storey brick-built hut. That was just the sort of place I was looking for.

I was painfully aware that my feet were crunching on the snow and leaving footprints, but I could think of nothing to do about that except to hope for more snow. The hut had a door at the side with a latch like the sort you sometimes see on garden gates. Full of hope, I tried it.

It was firmly locked. It was a solid wooden door and it didn't move at all. There was no way I could gain entry to the hut that way.

I walked all around the garages and all around the hut. There was not so much as a window in either. I walked round the garden, hoping for a summerhouse, a wooden gardening shed, anything. There was nothing. I walked all the way round the rectory, looking for open ventilator windows (although I do not know if I would have dared to break in) or anything at all that might give me a little shelter. Then I realised that there was nothing there for me. I was as firmly locked out as a street person looking for shelter in the stairwell of my block of flats at home would be.

The church clock struck seven. I was so cold that my teeth would not stop chattering, and my feet were numb. I knew I needed to find some shelter or I ran the risk of not surviving the night.

I had two remaining choices: the cottage or the church. I had no idea what condition the cottage was now in, I thought I had heard breaking glass when the men from the Jeeps first surrounded it, and if the windows were broken it would no longer be either warm or safe. The church was closer too. I decided to try it first, and only go back to the cottage if the church turned out to be no use.

I walked across the garden to the hedge and followed it round. Up ahead the ground started to slope and soon I was climbing again. I found a little gate in the hedge, but there was frozen snow that stopped it from opening. I climbed over it, and found myself in a lower part of the church yard. The huge old church loomed ahead of me, further up a steep path. I trudged towards it and saw at once a small door, the vestry I assumed. I tried it.

Of course, it was locked. I followed the church wall round, stepping several times into snow drifts that were up to my thighs. I was so cold it was hard to keep going. At last I reached the front of the church, where there was a porch. Snow had drifted into the porch and in the snow, even though it was so dark, I could see footprints. I tried the big wooden door, expecting it, also to be locked.

It wasn't. It groaned as I pushed it, but it opened, and I went in out of the wind and the snow.

181

My relief was enormous. I sat down on the first broken pew I came to, and took several deep breaths. It was still bitterly cold but there was no wind. My eyes adjusted a little to the darkness.

I suppose this church is no longer in use. It is huge, with a high arched roof, stone pillars, and an aisle which seemed, as I walked down it, either to consist of broken tiles, or to be covered in some sort of crunchy litter, wood or plaster from the ceiling, perhaps. I was looking for somewhere to hide but there was nothing. It was like a huge, empty barn with broken pews and very little else. I walked up to the choir area to see if I might be able to get into the vestry, and I did find a door, but it was locked. I stood and peered around me. It was very dark, even after my eyes had become accustomed to being inside, but it seemed to me there was nothing. I turned in a circle where I stood. Then I realised, my best bet was to shelter behind the altar.

I wished then I had brought a blanket with me. The floor was cold and hard, and felt dirty to the touch, but I did at least feel hidden. A little dim light filtered in from the window behind the altar, but I rooted around and found my torch. It felt safe to turn it on there. I opened my flask and drank the remaining coffee (it was cold) and ate the last of the boiled eggs. I thought I would write this journal. I knew I ought to, although to be honest I don't think I really felt like it, but my hands were stiff with cold. I decided that if I were to warm up I would need to move around, so I left my backpack where it was, and came out in front of the altar, and did a series of warm-up activities vaguely remembered from one of my earlier attempts at keeping fit. Then I settled back down, picked up my journal, and was about to start writing when I heard a vehicle in the road again, and then another. Then I realised how foolish I had been. If some group like the ATTF or even the ordinary police were really looking for me, they wouldn't just give up. Perhaps they had only driven the seven or eight miles to the nearest pub, had a meal and a drink or two, and had returned to renew their search. Or maybe it was a night shift… I felt desperate, and that is when I wrote the last diary entry. And I will be honest, I cried. I would have given almost anything to see Karl's face…

This morning, though, for some reason I feel better. I slept only in fits and starts and I was desperately cold. I have nothing left to eat. Today I think I need to get away. When Karl and I came back from buying my shopping we arrived back from the top of the valley. I am not sure, but I think we turned off a larger road. I have no idea what happens if I walk down the valley beyond the barn and the copse where I first saw the helicopter, so tonight, as soon as it is dark, I plan to head out for the main road. Perhaps there I will be able to hitch a lift. I need to get back to somewhere where there are houses, somewhere where there are homeless people among whom I can hide. In the mean time, perhaps I should spend some time thinking of my friends, and of what might be happening to them.

I feel as if I am a character in a book. I am sitting behind an altar in a redundant church, I am cold and hungry and I am filthy, but after all, I can worship anywhere …

Thursday 27ᵗʰ January 4.15pm.

How ridiculous of me to think I would walk out of here. I was woken from a doze just a minute or so ago by the sound of dogs barking. They are tracking me. It is only a matter of time before they find me, and I see no point in running or hiding, although I will put this journal up on the high windowsill behind the altar and cover it with dust and rubble. They may not find it. I can hear the helicopter too. I really cannot imagine what is going to happen now …

CHAPTER 5

Tuesday 1ˢᵗ February 2014 3.20am

Since I no longer have a journal, and they will not let me have any sort of notebook, I am writing this with the ink tube from the inside of a pen on the back of the paperwork they left in my cell yesterday. The paperwork tells me what is expected of me and details a list of sanctions if I don't toe the line. It is standard issue, and includes details of an earned incentive programme for which I, as a dangerous prisoner, am not eligible.

This is the third cell I have been in since the dogs found me in the church, and the fourth or fifth place of captivity, depending on how I categorise them. The dog handlers were indeed Welsh ATTF, and they did not formally arrest me. I heard them coming and stood in front of the altar in full sight as they smashed into the church with some sort of large guns aimed towards me like a bad movie or a child's DeV game. I didn't try to run or hide, there was no point, and they didn't speak to me except to shout "Hands behind your back!" as they cuffed me. Then they put some sort of black cotton bag over my head and led me out.

I was taken to the helicopter. It was my first ever ride in a helicopter, what a pity I couldn't see anything! Then after quite a short while they transferred me to a plane. The only time they removed my hood was when we had taken off and they gave me some water and a sort of fruit biscuit. I could see then that I was at the back of quite a large space, like a normal transatlantic plane with most of the seats taken out and the windows blackened. The chair on which I sat was comfortable enough, but one ankle was chained to the leg so that after a few hours it was really hard to avoid cramp. I had to use the loo with my head still covered, and the door open, and as far as I could tell from the small amount of conversation in my part of the plane and the uproarious laughter that came from further forward, all the officers were men. Personal dignity was obviously not a high priority for these people.

The flight was long. They had taken my watch and there was no way to tell how much time had passed, but I started to feel very sleepy a few hours after we took off and I assumed it was night-time in England. Of course I couldn't sleep properly but I dozed, and also sat awake for what seemed like hours. I tried to settle in the Light but I just couldn't. I wondered if Jo, Sabina and Imran had suffered the same treatment, and even wondered whether I might see them when I finally arrived wherever it was I was going. They brought me more water and very cold sandwiches with white bread and limp lettuce, and some meat I couldn't identify. I tried asking one officer where we were going but he just glared at me and made his way forward again, beyond the curtain, where the other men were, it seemed, playing cards.

When we left the plane it was into warm, humid air. All I could see was the tarmac under my feet, with white lines painted here and there. It was good to walk but my shoulders were aching from having my hands cuffed behind my back for a good hour before we reached our destination. I felt dirty too, and dazed, and I really wanted to spend some time on my own in a loo. I was pushed rather than helped into some sort of van, and driven away from wherever we had landed. My Welsh ATTF officers were no longer with me, all the accents now were American, mostly Southern drawls, but I don't know the US well enough to know which state I am in. We drove for maybe two hours, passed through some security and walked across more tarmac in sunshine and shade, through doors which were unlocked and locked again behind me, and which slid open like the doors in Simon's prison, and when finally they took the hood off my head I was in a room with breeze blocks painted light grey from the ceiling to about hip level and dark grey down to the floor, and with no window.

My days were a confusion of interviews and tests: blood tests, a 'use of English' test, an IQ test (I wonder how well I scored?) and a dental inspection with a white clad man who muttered about socialised medicine but who apparently found nothing wrong. I was allowed at last to shower and wash my hair but the soap made no bubbles and there was no shampoo, so that my hair feels lifeless. A large woman officer in the grey uniform which is already so familiar, and a bullet-proof waistcoat which they call a vest, interviewed me about my next of kin and filled in some sort of form on a pad of that old fashioned self-duplicating paper I remember from years ago. I was reluctant to give them Amy's contact details, I really don't want to bring any trouble down on her, so I just said that my brother and my parents are dead and the woman seemed too bored to pursue it. I was given a white jumpsuit and a white t-shirt to wear, along with some ragged and faintly stained underwear, and realised from the labels that, like Simon before me, I am a guest of the State of Texas. I was locked in one cell and then another, and each time they moved me a bag was put over my head. Sometimes I heard women calling out as I passed, once a globule of saliva landed on my cuffed wrist, and once I was actually taken outside, made once more to climb into a van, and transported to the place where I am now.

It was only this morning as I lay on this concrete shelf trying to ignore the crazy shouting of the woman in the next cell who seems to speak only Spanish, that the words 'extraordinary rendition' came into my head, and with those words the events of the last six months slotted into place. So now I am sitting in the half light, they dim the bulbs from eleven until three but it is never really dark, and trying to write my journal as I would at home, to settle myself, and to come to terms with what I think will happen. I do not expect to get out of here alive. Jo or Sabina might be very close to me, in a pod almost within shouting distance, but they might be anywhere else in the world. There is so much I do not know. Was Karl my friend or my enemy? Was Derek, the green-jacket man, a spy or a seeker? Do they, that anonymous 'they', really believe I am a threat or is something else going on here? But one thing I am sure about: now that they have brought me here I will never be freed. My story is one that they can never allow to be told.

I wonder if they serve warrants and put political prisoners on Death Watch, as they do criminals, or whether one day I will just be led away to be injected or shot?

I wonder what Amy will be told?

I wonder what will happen to my flat?

I feel very peaceful. I no longer need to run or hide, I no longer have to make any decisions. I just need to wait, and to learn to feel the presence of the Spirit in this world of steel and concrete. It shouldn't be too hard, or last too long.

EPILOGUE

I was a day too late returning to the cottage. By the time I arrived she was already out of the country. I booked a flight, and while I waited I arranged for the windows to be re-glazed and I cleaned up inside. Her possessions were neatly folded and stored and the place, apart from the damp where snow had blown in, was spotless. There was very little food left, just some frozen vegetables and the coffee. I might ask the owner if I can rent the cottage for a year, now that I am retiring. I found her journal on the church windowsill, and I have it now, stored safely where it cannot be discovered.

They let me visit once. We were separated by bullet proof glass and it was hard talking to her on the phone when I wanted to reach out to her, to offer some sort of personal warmth. She didn't look good. Her hair was lank and her face very pale, but she smiled that same old smile, a mixture of perplexity and something that might be joy. I never really understood her. She seemed to know what lay ahead, although I gathered they had not actually told her. I reassured her about Sabina and Imran who really were just deported, but I have no knowledge of Jo, and when I tried to find out my commanding officer said I had no need to know. I have no stomach to go on with this now, and he accepted my resignation without any protest.

In her journal she says that she opens herself to the Spirit and takes her direction from her own experiences. I have never believed this sort of thing, but now that I will have time, I think I will try it. Judging by the outcomes in her life, it seems like a fairly subversive activity.

The newspapers, those that reported it at all, talked about the 'just execution' of a 'known terrorist', and of making the world safe for democracy. They didn't let me witness the execution. I hope death came easily.

Perhaps, if I practice the business of holding things in the Light, I might find that I, too, need to help the destitute or work to correct some cruel injustice? It will be an interesting experiment.

I will not see Maria again. In fact I don't think I'll ever return to this country, or at least, not willingly.

My flight to England leaves within the hour.

I feel rather alone.